GARNET

GEMS OF WOLFE ISLAND THREE

HELEN HARDT

GARNET

Gems of Wolfe Island Three
Wolfes of Manhattan Eight
Helen Hardt

HARDT & SONS ♥

Paperback ISBN: 978-1-952841-10-1

PRINTED IN THE UNITED STATES OF AMERICA

HARDT & SONS ♥

For Eric, my editor!

ALSO BY HELEN HARDT

Trilogy One—Talon and Jade

Craving

Obsession

Possession

Trilogy Two—Jonah and Melanie

Melt

Burn

Surrender

Trilogy Three—Ryan and Ruby

Shattered

Twisted

Unraveled

Trilogy Four—Bryce and Marjorie

Breathless

Ravenous

Insatiable

Trilogy Five—Brad and Daphne

Fate

Legacy

Descent

Trilogy Six—Dale and Ashley

Awakened

Cherished

Freed

Trilogy Seven—Donny and Callie

Trusting Sydney

Tantalizing Maria

Standalone Novels and Novellas

Reunited

Misadventures:

Misadventures of a Good Wife (with Meredith Wild)

Misadventures with a Rockstar

The Cougar Chronicles:

The Cowboy and the Cougar

Calendar Boy

Daughters of the Prairie:

The Outlaw's Angel

Lessons of the Heart

Song of the Raven

Collections:

Destination Desire

Her Two Lovers

Non-Fiction:

got style?

PRAISE FOR HELEN HARDT

WOLFES OF MANHATTAN

"It's hot, it's intense, and the plot starts off thick and had me completely spellbound from page one."
~The Sassy Nerd Blog

"Helen Hardt...is a master at her craft."
~K. Ogburn, Amazon

"Move over Steel brothers... Rock is *everything!*"
~Barbara Conklin-Jaros, Amazon

"Helen has done it again. She winds you up and weaves a web of intrigue."
~Vicki Smith, Amazon

FOLLOW ME SERIES

"Hardt spins erotic gold..."

"22 Best Erotic Novels to Read"
~*Marie Claire* Magazine

"Intensely erotic and wildly emotional..."
~*New York Times* bestselling author Lisa Renee Jones

"With an edgy, enigmatic hero and loads of sexual tension, Helen Hardt's fast-paced Follow Me Darkly had me turning pages late into the night!"
~*New York Times* bestselling author J. Kenner

"Christian, Gideon, and now...Braden Black."
~Books, Wine, and Besties

"A tour de force where the reader will be pulled in as if they're being seduced by Braden Black, taken for a wild ride, and left wanting more."
~*USA Today* Bestselling Author Julie Morgan

"Hot. Sexy. Intriguing. Page-Turner. Helen Hardt checks all the boxes with *Follow Me Darkly!*"
~International Bestselling Author Victoria Blue

STEEL BROTHERS SAGA

"*Craving* is the jaw-dropping book you *need* to read!"
~*New York Times* bestselling author Lisa Renee Jones

"Completely raw and addictive."
~#1 *New York Times* bestselling author Meredith Wild

WARNING

The Gems of Wolfe Island series contains adult language and scenes, including flashbacks of physical and sexual abuse. Please take note.

PROLOGUE
ASPEN

In volleyball, the middle blocker controls the net.

It's a common misconception that you must be tall to play middle, though at six feet, I'm definitely tall for a woman. I was always tall for my age, which was a real pain in the ass until all the guys shot up during puberty.

I started playing volleyball when I was four years old. Because I was always the tallest, middle became my position, but I kept it not because of my height, but because I could jump.

I'm a damned good jumper.

You have to be able to jump to stop the opposing team's attacks. Then, on offense, jumping is essential for spiking and scoring.

I was good.

I was damned good. The best, even.

I lost count, during all my years of play, how many times I got hoisted on my teammates' shoulders for scoring the winning point in a match.

It never got old.

Jumping. Blocking. Spiking. Staying in the ultimate physical condition because I spent the most time in the air.

Those were my jobs. I never set the ball. Other team members set it to me. As middle, I relied on my team members more than any other position.

On the island, though, I was on my own.

No team members to set me up.

I had to play offense, defense, and everything in between.

And my height wasn't a barrier to those men, as it was to many before. No. Those men loved my height, my athleticism.

I was a favorite to hunt. I made them feel like big bad dudes. What a blast to their ego when they took down Garnet, the star athlete.

I've got the scars to prove it.

No teammates to set me up.

I was on my own, so eventually I learned to go to that place in my head. The place where I was being hoisted up for winning the match for my team.

I loved being the best.

My team depended on me, and I never let them down.

Maybe I got a little full of myself.

Sometimes I almost have to laugh at the irony of it all.

After a couple of weeks on that island? I was no longer full of myself.

No.

I would've given up all my athletic ability, all my wins, all those times being hoisted up on others' shoulders...

Just to go home again.

The nightmares still come, although not as frequently. I live in Manhattan now, in the building the Wolfe family set up for all their father's victims. There are three other women here—Katelyn, Lily, and Kelly.

I don't know Lily and Kelly very well, but I had coffee with Katelyn. She's nice, although we don't have a lot in common. She and I had very different experiences on the island. She was humiliated more than brutalized.

Not to say what happened to her wasn't horrific. It was. And she *was* hunted. One time I remember—she came back used and beaten, and Diamond took care of her for weeks. Katelyn was different after that. Tougher. More rigid.

Me? I had to be tough the whole time. Offense and defense with no team to set me up.

And it still wasn't enough.

1

BUCK

"Moreno," I say into the phone.

I already know who it is. Reid Wolfe. Calling from Manhattan. I'm in LA, having just helped take down Kingsford Winston, one of the most dangerous drug lords in the city.

This was personal.

I was looking for his right-hand man, Lucifer Raven. The man who abused my sister.

I found him—or the man who used to be him, anyway.

Lucifer Ashton the third, or Luke as he likes to be called now. I never thought a man like him could change, but I saw it. Saw it with my own eyes.

Part of me still wants to sink a knife into his heart, but I'm done killing.

I did enough of that when I was on tour.

"It's me," Reid says. "We've got a problem."

"Another one?" I say with a touch of sarcasm.

"I'm serious. Where the fuck *are* you?"

I don't like his tone. I work for the Wolfe family, but I'm a contractor, not an employee. I don't have to report to him or anyone.

"I'm in LA. Who's asking?"

"I am. One of our girls, Aspen, is missing."

"What about Katelyn?" I ask, already knowing the answer.

"She's in LA. With her parents."

"And with Luke. Also known as Lucifer Charles Ashton the third. Street name Lucifer Raven."

Silence for a moment.

Then, "What the hell are you talking about?"

"She's safe. This man she was dating... Luke Johnson, the waiter? Surely you know who he really is."

"I do now. Are you telling me *two* of our women are missing?"

"No. She's safe. In love, apparently."

"For God's sake."

I'm not sure what to say. Katelyn Brooks fell in love with the man who abused my sister. Except he's changed. So he says. So Katelyn says.

"You sure she's safe?"

Am I sure? Hell, no. I don't trust Raven or Lucifer or Luke or whoever the hell he is this week, but Katelyn does. Katelyn is sure.

"For now," I say simply.

"All right," Reid says. "In the meantime, we do have a missing woman. Aspen Davis. Garnet from the island. I need you on it."

Good. A job will help.

"What do you need?"

"I need you to find her. She's gone, Buck. Zee is beside herself. We told these women we'd protect them. Keep them safe. And Aspen just... She just disappeared into thin air."

"I'm on it."

"You'll be paid handsomely. Your usual rate. Find her. Please, Buck."

"What resources do I have?"

"Anything you need. Anything. Anything you fucking need."

"You got it. I've got some buddies who might be able to help as well."

"Absolutely. And once you find her, you give her whatever she wants. Make her happy. Whatever she needs."

"Got it. I'm on."

My next phone call is to Phoenix. Leif Ramsey, who also works for the Wolfes. We served together, and we've always had each other's backs. In fact, we're the only two survivors from our last tour.

"Hey, Buck," Ramsey says.

"Phoenix, I'm going to need you. The Wolfes have a missing woman."

"Man, that family can't catch a break."

"Tell me about it."

"Any luck on the Raven?"

I don't answer right away.

"Buck?"

"The Raven no longer exists. He's Luke now. Luke Johnson."

"You found him then?"

"I did. And..."

It's not easy for me to say. I don't forgive him. I'll never forgive him. Never did I think he could change. A leopard doesn't change its spots, right?

"What?"

"He's alive. And with full immunity."

"Are you fucking kidding me?"

"I'm not. I'll explain it all to you when I see you. Get to Manhattan as soon as you can. We've got a woman to find."

2

ASPEN

No. This can't be happening again. I won't let it happen again.

But it *is* happening.

All I wanted was to go home. To see the mountains of Colorado. Maybe say hi to my family.

So I left Manhattan, and I didn't tell anyone where I was going. Why should I? I'm a free citizen of this country. I don't owe anyone anything.

I don't have a credit card, so I paid cash for my train ticket. I was supposed to arrive at Union Station in Denver tomorrow.

Instead?

I'm alone.

Alone. In the dark. In a locked room.

At least they didn't take my clothes this time.

How is this even happening?

I jerk out of my thoughts when someone knocks on the door.

"Go away," I say.

"Are you decent?" A man's voice.

"Go *away*."

A click. The door opens.

I dart my gaze around, looking for something to use as a weapon. In desperation, I grab the bible from the night table.

Softcover. Damn.

"Hey." The man enters. "You want some food?"

"Could you just let me out of here? Please?"

"Yeah. We're going back to Manhattan."

"But I don't—"

"Aspen," he says. "The Wolfes are worried about you."

"Tell them I'm fine. I just want to see Colorado. I want to see the beauty of my state. The Rockies. The snowcapped mountains. The gorgeous colors."

He's handsome, this man. And why that occurs to me I have no idea. He doesn't respond right away. I clutch the bible to my chest.

"All right," he says finally. "I'll take you."

He'll take me? And I'm just supposed to trust him? He says he works for the Wolfes. I could easily find out, except he took my phone.

"Who the hell are you?" For some reason, holding the bible gives me courage. "Why did you pull me off that train?"

"Because we thought you were in danger. The Wolfes thought you were in danger."

"I'm not in danger. I just wanted—"

"I get it. I do. But you left without telling anyone, and there was no way to trace your ticket."

"Because I paid in cash. I don't have a credit card. It's nothing. I wasn't even gone very long."

"True enough. But you need to let the Wolfes know when you're leaving. They freaked out."

"Look. The Wolfe family got me off that island. But it was also the Wolfe family that got me *on* that island in the first place."

"That was their father, Derek Wolf. Reid and his siblings are good people."

"I appreciate—"

"Do you? Because if you appreciated it, you would've let them know you were leaving. They freaked out, Aspen. They put me on the case."

"So you kidnapped me? Me? When you know my history?"

"I did what I was paid to do. I got you to safety. For all I knew at the time, you had been taken against your will and put on that train again."

"Well, now you know that's not the case, Mister"

"Moreno. Antonio Moreno. But I'm called Buck."

"Mr. Buck."

"Just Buck."

I swallow. For the first time, I look at him. Really look at him. He's tall, at least three inches taller than I am, and I'm no slouch at six feet. Muscled, dark hair, and dark eyes.

A few tingles shoot through me.

Tingles I wasn't sure I'd ever feel again.

"Please," I say. "Let me go home. Let me go to Colorado."

His dark eyes soften. "I'll talk to the Wolfes."

"I'm a free agent, you know. The Wolfes don't own me. Nobody fucking owns me."

"Of course no one owns you. The Wolfes are just trying to protect you. They were worried."

Sadness whips through me. He's right, of course. Reid Wolfe and his wife, Zee, have been nothing but kind to me. They've bent over backwards to make sure I have everything I need, and all they asked in return is that I stay safe. Stay protected. Check in and out with the security guard when I leave.

And I didn't do that.

I didn't do that because I needed to take myself back. I needed to take ownership of my own body and soul.

For so long, on that island, I was someone else's property to use and abuse.

And I've got scars to prove it.

I was beaten.

Raped.

Hunted.

They had weapons. I did not.

All I had was my brain and my strong body.

Sometimes I escaped.

Most of the time...I didn't.

Like I said, they had weapons.

And as strong and fit as I was, more often than not, I was captured and abused.

I was a favorite on the hunting ground. Diamond told me it was because I was a natural athlete, tall, muscular.

"And beautiful," she used to say. "They want to take you because you're beautiful."

I never considered myself beautiful. And on the island? Any beauty I possessed was a fucking curse.

Katelyn—now *she's* beautiful. Blond, fair, light blue eyes.

Soft and delicate.

That's feminine beauty.

Me? I'm more masculine than feminine.

Standing here next to Buck, though, I feel more feminine than I have in a long time.

He so tall, so broad. He dwarfs me, and that's not an easy thing to do.

He grabs his phone out of his pocket, punches on it, and then places it to his ear. "Hey, it's Moreno."

Pause.

"She wants to go to Colorado. Says she wants to see her state. Remember its beauty."

Pause.

"Absolutely. You got it."

Pause.

"Right. Got it. Bye."

Buck turns to me. "We're going. We're going to go to Colorado."

"*We?*"

"That's right, Aspen. If you insist on going to Colorado, I'm going with you, to ensure your safety."

3

BUCK

Chaperoning Aspen on a trip to Colorado is no hardship. The woman is freaking gorgeous.

Plus, I'm making a cool two grand per hour to babysit.

No complaints here.

I'd been ready to pull out all the stops, put my training to use to find a kidnapping victim. I called in Leif—Phoenix—and told him to bring in the battalion. I called him off an hour ago, as I don't need him.

Turns out? Aspen left on her own.

I can't blame her. She *wants* to be on her own. She was held captive for five years on that damned island.

And I know a little about captivity.

More than a little, actually, and it's stuff I'd much rather forget.

"We'll rent a car," I say. "We'll be there by tomorrow."

"Can we fly?"

"If you'd rather."

She pauses, seeming to ponder. "No, a car's good. The idea of being at an airport is kind of..."

"I get it."

"We were flown from the island on the Wolfes' private jet. I haven't been to an airport in... Well, a while."

"Whatever you want."

"It's just... I was on a trip, to a championship game. That was the last time I was at an airport. I was taken when I was at the hotel."

She doesn't have to say any more. I get it.

"You don't have to talk about it."

"Good. I wasn't going to. But yeah, no airports."

So that's why she chose the train. I figured it was because it was cheaper, but I should know better. The Wolfes are taking care of these ladies. They probably have as much cash as they want at their disposal.

"A car it is then," I say.

"Good."

"Get ready. I've been instructed to get you whatever you need. Take a shower or whatever."

"Okay."

"I'll go take care of the car, and then we'll be on our way."

Taking care of the car is easy. Easy as calling Reid Wolfe's assistant. She's out of the office, apparently, so I get his secretary, Alicia.

"Not a problem, Mr. Moreno," Alicia says. "I'll get the car delivered to you within the hour."

"Delivered to me?"

"Yeah, someone will drive it to your hotel."

Right. I should've known. Top-notch service for the Wolfes. An hour later, a Lincoln sedan arrives, and I have the keys. I also have my Wolfe credit card, which I'm to use for all expenses when I'm on their service.

I have no idea what the credit limit is, but I know it's high, because I've put some damned high expenses on it in the past.

I knock on Aspen's door. She opens it slowly and peeks out.

"All set," I say. "The car's here."

She pulls her suitcase out of the room.

I grab it from her. "I'll take that."

"Oh. Sure. Thanks."

We make our way down to the car, a bellhop secures our luggage, then we're on our way.

"We'll be there by dinnertime," I say.

"Okay."

"Where do you want to go first?" I ask her. "Your parents' house?"

She doesn't say anything.

"I get it. It will be a little difficult to explain my presence."

"No, it's not that. Well, at least, it's not *all* that."

"Have you seen them since you were rescued?"

"Actually, I haven't."

I can't help it. I lift my eyebrows. "Why not?"

"It's complicated."

"Honey, life is rarely easy."

I hate myself as soon as I say the words.

My life sure as hell hasn't been easy, but that doesn't negate the fact hers has been truly hellacious. I need to stop thinking that everyone has had it better than I have, because it's not true.

I joined the SEALs. I knew what might await me, and I

went in headfirst. I was all ego—all ego that eventually got shattered.

This woman though? She was a championship volleyball player. She didn't ask for what she got.

"I'm sorry," I say.

"For what?"

"I didn't mean to make light of... Well, you know."

"It's okay."

"Do your parents know what you've been through?"

"They know."

"And they haven't wanted to see you?"

"Oh, they have. I'm the one that put the kibosh on it. I didn't want to see them. But it's not what you think."

"I'm not thinking anything, Aspen."

"Aren't you? You not thinking I'm some kind of spoiled little brat who's decided she doesn't need her parents?"

"God, no. I don't have any preconceived notions about you. I'm just really sorry you've been through so much."

She draws in a deep breath, shakes her head. "I don't want you to be sorry for me."

"Okay."

"I'm serious. You don't know what it's like. Having everyone pity you for what you went through."

"Actually, honey, I know exactly what that's like." No lie there. It sucks.

She turns then. Out of the corner of my eye, I can see that she's staring at me, wondering what I've been through.

I'm not about to enlighten her. No more than she's going to enlighten me about what she's been through.

The difference is that I know what happened on that island. I've got a pretty good idea of what she's been through, and it's not pretty. Far from it. It's fucking hideous.

She, however, *doesn't* know my past. She doesn't know the horrors I've seen, the horrors I've endured.

Best to keep it that way, for both our sakes.

"There is someone I need to see," she says.

"Whatever you need. Just give me her name."

"*His* name," she says. "Brandon Page. He was... He was my fiancé."

4

ASPEN

I haven't been in touch with Brandon, and I asked my parents not to contact him. Whether they abided by my wishes I have no idea. I wouldn't put it past my mother to talk to him without my permission. It's kind of her thing. She loved Brandon. Heck, I'm pretty sure she loved him more than she loved me. Okay, that's not true, but she loved him as much as she loved me for sure.

Brandon and I...

At the time, I thought he was the love of my life.

When I was taken, I was sure he'd come for me.

I was wrong.

I don't fault him. No one could have found me. I know that now. But I had to erase him from my mind. I had to forgive him for not coming for me.

To make it through, I had to rely on myself and myself only.

No Brandon.

No teammates.

No one.

No one but Aspen.

No one but Garnet.

They called me Garnet because of a cherry angioma birthmark on the top of my left breast. It was an unwritten rule on the island that none of the men mar that mark—that mark that made me Garnet.

It never bothered me. It's not huge or anything, about the size of a pea.

But now? I'll be getting rid of it as soon as I can. Cherry angiomas are benign, but I'm going to have it excised from my body.

I want no memory of Garnet.

I want no memory of that island.

Already, I've begun to forget. It's like I've willed it.

The nightmares still come. The only difference is that I don't remember them when I wake up. But I don't need to remember to know what they were.

The feelings are the same.

The dread, the horror. The pure fright.

My body knows. My body remembers even if my mind does not.

I'll go back to Manhattan eventually. Back to group. Back to private sessions with Macy, our therapist.

But I need Colorado.

I need the open air.

I need the mountains.

I need to see Brandon.

I need to find out if he still wants me.

Do I want him?

I wish I knew.

I'm hoping that seeing him will spur some kind of

emotion in me. Because right now? I'm totally devoid of emotion.

I'm an empty shell.

My body may have tingled slightly—and I mean *slightly* —at the sight of Buck Moreno, but it was only my body.

I felt nothing emotionally. Absolutely nothing.

And frankly?

That scares me more than the worst night on that damned island.

5

BUCK

"A fiancé?" I say.

She clears her throat. "Yes."

"And you haven't spoken to him?"

"I haven't. I haven't been able to. I don't expect you to understand."

Again, I understand more than she knows.

A hint of what feels kind of like jealousy spikes into my gut. I hardly know this woman. She's beautiful, yes, but I have no reason to feel anything for her other than physical attraction.

Plus, why would I worry about a fiancé? She hasn't seen or talked to him in five years. He could be married with a kid by now.

"We'll find him," I say dryly.

"Thank you. I'd like to see him before I see my parents."

"Whatever you want."

My only job is to take care of her, see to her needs, and the Wolfes are paying me handsomely for it.

We make it to Denver by five p.m.

"Are you hungry?" I ask.

"I don't really get hungry anymore."

Again, I understand more than she knows.

"Still, you have to eat. Does anything at all sound good?"

"Whatever you like is fine."

"Italian food," I say. "Though it's always disappointing, as no one makes it the way my mother can."

"Your mother's Italian?"

I can't help a chuckle. "My name is Antonio Moreno."

"Right. Yes. But your mother could still be...something else."

"Her maiden name is Giovanni. First name Marina."

"Marina Moreno?"

I chuckle again. "Yup. My father's name is Antonio Senior, and my sister's name is Emilia, but we call her Emily. I have a little brother too. Giovanni, from my mom's maiden name, but we call him Johnny."

"I see."

Not exactly sure why I'm giving her my family history. She certainly didn't ask for it. But yes, I do love Italian food, and even though it's never as good as my mother's, it's still what I always go for.

"So Italian?" I say again.

"Sure. That's fine. I'll have spaghetti and meatballs or something."

"Lasagna is my favorite. But no one makes it like—"

"Your mother can. Right."

I sigh. Maybe I shouldn't try to get her to talk. After all, there was a time when I didn't talk to anyone either.

"You know Denver better than I do," I say. "What's the best Italian place in town?"

"Honestly, I don't know. I went to college in Boulder, and I haven't been back since…"

Damn. I'm so not good at this. You'd think I'd be better, having been through my own trauma.

"Not a problem. That's what Google is for." I hand her my phone. "Find something for us."

She takes the phone and starts typing.

"Anything?" I ask.

"Yeah. There's a place two miles from here called Fornetti's. It has mostly five-star reviews."

"Fornetti's it is. Put it in the GPS."

Ten minutes later, I'm handing the rental car off to a valet.

We enter the restaurant, and I gape a little. I was expecting a quaint place with checkered tablecloths and taper candles in empty straw-covered Chianti bottles with Dean Martin crooning "That's Amore" in the background. Instead, we walk into an elegant dining room with tuxedo-clad waitstaff, classic white table coverings, and no Dean Martin. Just soft string music provided by a violinist who walks table to table.

"Wow." Aspen widens her eyes as well. "I didn't realize it was this nice of a place. I'm not sure I'm properly dressed."

"You look great."

No lie there. She may only be wearing skinny jeans, loafers, and a sweater, but she looks amazing. Hot, actually, but I need to keep that thought way in the back of my mind.

I'm wearing jeans, military boots, and a button-down shirt. I guess we'll find out quickly if they let us in.

"Good evening, sir," the host, also tuxedo-clad, says. "Do you have reservations?"

"I'm afraid not. We just got into town. Do you have a table for two available?"

"Actually, yes, you're in luck." He makes some markings on a chart in front of him. "Sandra, could you show them to table twenty-five?"

Sandra, who looks about twelve but is still wearing a tux, grabs two menus. "Of course. Follow me please."

Table twenty-five turns out to be in the back. Dark and secluded.

I hold the seat out for Aspen.

Sandra hands us the menus. "Jeremy will be your server. He'll be with you shortly."

I open my menu and inhale. Damn, the prices.

But it's all on the Wolfes. They've told me more than once never to worry about costs. Reid reiterated as much this morning about Aspen. I'm to spare no expense to show her what she needs to see. I assume that means dining.

"What looks good?" I ask.

"My God..." Aspen's eyes are wide.

"I know, but don't worry about the cost."

"The Wolfes have already spent so much money on me."

"They owe you. For what their father did to you. Please don't worry about any of it."

She looks down at her menu but doesn't say anything.

Lasagna of course is on the menu. And it's not inexpensive. That's what I'll order. It's what I always order.

Jeremy, also in a tux with slicked back blond hair, arrives to take drink orders.

"Nothing for me," I say. "I'm driving. Aspen?"

She shakes her head. "Just some water would be wonderful."

"Make that two," I say to Jeremy.

The truth is, I don't drink much, although Leif and I have

been known to occasionally tie one on. I drank a lot when I got back from my last tour. To try to numb the pain.

What I found out eventually though was numbing the pain doesn't do any good. Because the pain is still there when the numbness wears off.

The pain is *always* there.

A few minutes later, Jeremy brings our waters. "Any appetizers?"

"How about some calamari?" I ask Aspen.

"Sure. Whatever you'd like."

"Calamari," I say. "And I'll have the lasagna."

"Are you ready to order your entrée, ma'am?" Jeremy asks.

"Sure. Spaghetti and meatballs, please."

I don't know why I'm surprised. That's what she said she was going to order. Jeremy makes a few notes on his pad and then leaves us alone again.

"So tell me about this Brandon," I say.

"I would if I could. It's been over five years since I've seen him."

"There must be a reason why you didn't want to contact him once you were found."

"There is. I... I'm not the same person I was."

"I understand."

"Do you?"

"With all due respect, Aspen, yes, I do. I was a Navy SEAL. I did three tours in Afghanistan. I've seen more than anyone should have to see. Experienced more than anyone should have to experience. And while I don't pretend to know exactly what you've been through and exactly how it's all affected you, I do understand trauma."

So much for not burdening her with my problems.

She nods.

"It's okay," I say. "We don't have to talk."

"Good. Thank you for understanding." She takes a sip of water.

This meal will be long.

But it's okay. I don't mind looking at Aspen. She's very beautiful, with dark hair cut short—really short—brown eyes, and minimal makeup. Not that she needs any at all. And her body... I'm feeling something. I'm not exactly sure what, but it's been a long time since that part of me has felt anything.

Anything at all.

6

ASPEN

"**M**arry me," Brandon says.

We'd just won a match and were bound for the championship, and I was on the shoulders of my teammates, when Brandon came down from the stands and got down on one knee.

My teammates cheer. Were they in on this?

Happiness—the elation of it all—surged through me. I was already high on adrenaline from the game.

I never expected this. Brandon and I haven't talked about marriage. But I'm on fucking cloud nine. Nope. Make that cloud ninety-nine.

And this beautiful man is on one knee before me. Before me and my teammates.

"Oh my God, yes!" I scream.

My teammates lower me to the ground where my legs wobble and I nearly lose my footing. Luckily the girls are there to steady me.

Brandon opens the velvet box he's holding. A gold band with a small diamond solitaire perched on it stares back at me. Brandon *and I are young. This is what he can afford, and that means the world to me.*

I lift my left hand, and he removes the ring and places it on my finger.

"Perfect fit," he says. "Just like us."

❧

I ALWAYS TOOK my ring off for games, but I put it back on after I left the locker room.

I was wearing it when I was taken.

When I woke up, of course, it was gone. I was naked, trapped in some kind of concrete dungeon, where I had to fight for my life.

They called me "worthy prey."

In fact, they called me the worthiest prey they'd seen.

At the time, in my still champion state, I considered their words a compliment in some warped way.

Turned out, it wasn't a compliment. When I ended up on that island, running for my life every night, it wasn't a compliment.

I suppose I wasn't actually running for my life.

They weren't allowed to kill us. But they could do pretty much anything else. Many times I was beaten beyond recognition, and I have the scars to prove it. I've been whipped, cut, stabbed, mutilated.

Oddly, my face remained unscathed. Sure, they punched me, gave me a few black eyes, a few swollen lips, but all those wounds healed without scars.

When I'm wearing clothes, no one can see what I've been through. My face looks exactly the same.

Except for my eyes.

When I look into my eyes in the mirror, I see what was done to me, even though I don't let myself remember a lot of it, and I assume everyone else can see it as well.

Buck's calamari arrives, and he offers me some. I decline, still sipping my water.

"You sure? Smells great."

"I'm sure."

Squid? No thanks. We were fed a lot of seafood on the island, and I prefer not to eat it now. Katelyn told me the same thing. Strangely, I never ate red meat before. Only poultry, fish, and vegetables.

Now? Red meat is all I eat, it seems.

It's filling, and it doesn't matter that I never really cared for the taste before I was taken. I don't taste anything now, anyway.

Buck fills his appetizer plate with the fried squid. He dips it in marinara and brings a piece to his mouth.

And I can't help but think about how exquisite he is.

His lips are full, and he has several days of black stubble on his jawline.

He's all muscle, and naked he must be...

A surge of arousal grips me.

How strange to feel something like this. Mere months ago, I swore no man would ever touch me, but this man...

He's been kind to me, and once I found out he was no threat, I've felt nothing but safe with him. Even though he's huge and full of muscles and could easily overpower me, I feel safe. Protected.

The men on the island weren't anything like Buck. Men like Buck don't need to abuse women to feel powerful. Men like Buck are powerful on their own.

"Can I ask a question?"

He swallows his bite of calamari. "I think you just did."

"All right. Can I ask you another question after this one?"

"Ask me whatever you want, Aspen. I can't guarantee I'll answer."

"Fair enough." I finish my water, let it glide down my throat. "You said your name is Antonio. Why are you called Buck?"

"It was my nickname as a kid, but then it became my SEAL name on my last tour as well."

"Why was it your nickname? It doesn't really go with Antonio."

"Right. But my father's name was also Antonio, and my parents wanted to be able to differentiate us, so they started calling me Buck."

"Okay...but that still doesn't exactly tell me why."

"That's the only reason I know."

He looks down, continues with his calamari.

7

BUCK

I'm lying, of course. I know why my parents used to call me Buck. It means robust and spirited, like the male deer called a buck.

I was a robust and spirited young kid. Stubborn to a fault, always moving. I ran everywhere. Never walked. I was always full of energy, and I channeled that energy into sports. When I didn't get the scholarship I wanted for football, I joined the Navy instead.

In some ways the best decision I ever made.

In other ways—the worst.

The name Buck, although it's been with me since I was a kid, is now synonymous with my last tour. There were six guys on that assignment, and only two of us returned—Phoenix and me.

I took the most chances, the most risks.

I should've died.

Or...instead of taking all the risks, I should've been protecting my buddies. Shielding them from danger. Instead, I was risking my own life.

How I made it out alive, I'll never know.

I was a sniper. A crack shot. I never missed.

Phoenix said they should call me Crack. The guys laughed. Crack. Butt crack. Ass crack.

I tackled Phoenix to the ground. Then I looked around at the rest of them and said, "It's Buck. Call me fucking Buck."

So they did. And they never laughed about me being a crack shot again. I saved their asses many times.

Until I didn't.

"It's a male deer," Aspen says. "That's what a buck is."

"True."

"It's a cool name. A strong name."

"Yeah, well, it's a hell of a lot better than Antonio." *Or Crack.*

"Tell me something about yourself," she says.

"What do you want to know?"

"I don't care. I just want to talk about something. Try to keep my mind from going places I don't want to go."

"I understand."

Do I ever.

"I told you about my family. That I was a SEAL."

"Why'd you leave the military?" she asks.

"My tour was over."

God, please don't let her ask about the tour...

"Guess what I was named for."

Whew. No more military questions.

"The Aspen trees in Colorado," I say.

She smiles then. A beautiful smile. An almost mischievous smile.

"That's what everybody thinks, I'm actually named after my mother's maiden name. Her name is Lisa Jane Aspen."

"Oh? And then of course you're from Colorado..."

"Right? Everybody thinks it's the trees."

"Funny. My little brother has my mother's maiden name as well."

"Right, you said that." She shrugs. "I don't know why that didn't occur to me when you told me."

"Because you have a lot of other stuff on your mind. Do you have any brothers and sisters?"

"Nope. I'm an only child. My parents' one and only. Unfortunately, when my mom had me, she had some nasty bleeding, and they had to remove her uterus."

Wow. That totally sucks. "I'm sorry."

"They always said I was enough."

I can imagine why. She's an amazing specimen of woman. Tall, muscular, beautiful. A star athlete.

Damn. She's a lot like me.

Except she got her scholarship. I know all about her history from the Wolfes. Of course, volleyball scholarships are easier to come by than football scholarships. At least Division I football scholarships, which is what I wanted. I was competing with the best of the best.

Apparently I didn't measure up.

At six feet three inches and two hundred and seventy pounds, I was actually considered small for the defensive tackle position that I played.

But that was so long ago. Fifteen years now. Fifteen years and three tours later...

"Tell me something else," she says.

"I've been working for the Wolfes, freelancing for a couple years."

"How did you get that gig?"

"My buddy Leif and I came back from our last tour, and we were..."

Fucked up. That's what I want to say, but I don't want her asking questions. We were getting some help for our PTSD, and one of our therapists mentioned that the Wolfes were hiring for independent security.

"...looking for work," I continue. "We heard Reid Wolfe was hiring for security, so we went to see him."

"Oh. That's good. Right?"

"Yeah. Good."

It is, in its way. The Wolfes pretty much give us carte blanche. We're allowed to break laws, as long as we cover our tracks and keep a low profile.

Of course, ex-Navy SEALs can hardly keep a low profile.

We take up every room we enter.

But if there's one thing we're good at—besides taking up a room—it's leaving no trace. I haven't broken a lot of laws since I've been back on American soil. The few I have broken have been negligible.

I'll never be caught because I'm that good at covering my tracks. And even when I'm not? The Wolfes' money is *very* good at covering my tracks.

I'm thankful when our food arrives. I'm tired of talking. I don't particularly like talking about myself, because so much of who I was got left overseas.

And I don't tell anybody those stories.

Not my parents, not my brother, not my sister.

And certainly not the beautiful women sitting in front of me.

I can't lay that on her—not after everything she's been through.

So I smile at her, pick up my fork, and cut off a piece of my lasagna. I stuff it in my mouth and chew. As usual, it's nothing compared to my mother's, but I take another bite.

And I relish not talking.

8

ASPEN

"I have the address," Buck says to me after he pays our check. "I assume you told your parents you were coming."

He assumes. Interesting. No one should assume anything about me. Hell, *I* don't know what I'm going to do between one moment and the next. How can anyone else?

"I haven't."

He raises his eyebrows. "Oh?"

"Funny. I left Manhattan, just got on a freaking train. I was ready to come here. But I never thought about what I would do once I got here."

"But you came to see your family, right? To see Brandon?"

"Part of me did, yes."

"And the other part of you?"

"I just wanted to be here. In Colorado. I wanted to see my mountains. Feel the open air."

"That's kind of hard to do in downtown Denver." He smiles.

I return his smile, and I'm amazed at how easy it is. "Yes. You get it, don't you?"

"I think so. We'll get a hotel for the night. Tomorrow we can regroup. I'll take you wherever you want to go. If you want to your parents, that's where we'll go. If you want to see Brandon, I'll find him for you, and that's where we'll go. But if you just want to see the mountains…"

"That's where we'll go?"

"Absolutely, Aspen. That's where we'll go." He pulls his phone out of his pocket, starts typing. "I can get us a couple rooms at The Four Seasons. It's a few buildings down."

"Perfect," I say.

I'm not sure I've ever stayed at The Four Seasons. When I was traveling with the volleyball team, we were treated well, but we were never put up at the best hotel in town. In fact… that last place… Someone took me right out of there.

"All right. Our rooms are reserved."

"Already? That was quick."

"The Wolfe name gets things done. You ready?"

I nod.

"I'll just leave the car in the valet parking for now. We'll walk."

"Okay."

He lets me lead as we leave the restaurant, but it feels all wrong. He's just being a gentleman, but even though this is my city, I feel…out of place. So much has changed in five and a half years. Even in downtown Denver.

This restaurant—it used to be a place called Palomino.

Not that I ever went there.

But I did spend a lot of time on the Sixteenth Street Mall, hanging out with friends, shopping. We saw a few shows at the Paramount Theater, ate at the Paramount Café.

Then we'd get on the bus and head back to Boulder, to campus.

Buck and I enter the hotel and walk across the marble lobby. Buck checks us in and hands me a key card.

"We're on the tenth floor."

I nod.

"Do you want to do anything? The bar's open. We can get a drink. They have an indoor pool. You feel like a swim?"

A swim.

That would take the edge off.

"I don't have a suit with me."

"There's a gift shop," Buck says. "We can get you a suit."

"No. I don't think so."

"Okay."

I shrug. "Not a drink either. I think I just want to go to my room."

"Absolutely."

What time is it anyway? I grab my phone out of my purse. "It's only eight o'clock." I laugh.

"Hey. Whatever you want. Those are my orders. Whatever you want."

A blanket of warmth coats me. Again, this man makes me feel sheltered. Comforted. Protected.

He leads me to the elevator, and we ascend to the tenth floor. Our rooms are next to each other, and he takes my key card from me and opens the door. He pulls my small carry-on in and sets it by the bed.

"There's a minibar if you get hungry or thirsty. Help yourself. It's all taken care of."

"Thank you." I notice the door on the side of our wall. "Adjoining rooms?"

"Yes. If you need me, I'm just a wall away."

I nod. "I'll be okay."

"Let me give you my number."

I grab my phone out of my purse and hand it to him. "Just program it in."

He does so and hands it back to me. "Anything," he says, enunciating. "I mean *anything*, Aspen. You just call. Or pound on the door. Or yell. Whatever."

Funny. Does he really think I'm going to yell in a hotel room?

"I'll call you if I need anything," I promise.

"Be sure you do." He rakes his gaze over me for a moment.

A moment that makes me extremely uncomfortable.

And...not so uncomfortable.

Bizarre. How can I be having any of these feelings?

It's because I find him a comfort. That's all it is.

"I will."

He nods again, but he doesn't smile. He simply turns, and I watch him from my doorway as he opens the door next to mine.

He enters his room and closes the door behind him.

I let my door close finally with a soft click, and then I look around the room.

I'm no stranger to hotel rooms.

The memories are so...jumbled. I had to block them out to deal with the trauma, but now, Macy says I'm going to need to access them. I'm going to need to remember all of them if I want to heal fully.

But maybe healing fully is overrated.

Maybe I just need to exist, to get through life, and not remember. Isn't not remembering a *good* thing? When what I've been through is so...

I cut my memories off.

I head to the bathroom, take a quick piss, and notice the amazing Jacuzzi tub. Lavender bath salts sit in the corner.

When did I last have a bath?

There's a shower in my apartment in Manhattan—a nice shower, but only a shower. We only had showers on the island in the dorms. And at the retreat center, we also only had showers.

A bath.

I'm not sure I've had a bath in twenty years.

Not since my mom used to give me baths.

That ended when I was what... Six? Seven?

Maybe even five?

And that's the problem. The problem Macy tells me about. When you start blocking out the bad memories, you end up blocking out the good ones as well.

I did have a pretty nice childhood. My parents wanted only me.

I turn the faucet on the tub.

A nice lavender salt bath.

That's what I'd like.

I sprinkle the salts into the pouring water. Lavender steam wafts over me, and I inhale. It's fragrant. A lovely scent, but isn't it supposed to be relaxing?

Relaxation, Macy always says, is more than just a nice smell.

It has to come from within. You don't have to force it, she says, but you do have to let it happen.

That's my problem. I've never been a person who just lets things happen. On the island, I fought and I fought and I fought, even when it would've been easier to give in.

I made it worse for myself a lot of times. They wanted me to give in. They hurt me more the more I fought.

I shed my clothes. They lie in a heap on the tile floor, and I stand in front of the full-length mirror on the back of the door.

I don't see Aspen.

I see Garnet.

I may not have scars on my face, but they're all over my body. A diagonal scar slices across my left breast. Right through my areola.

My other breast looks even weirder. I don't have a nipple. It was...

It was bitten off, resulting some of the worst pain I've ever experienced.

Reconstructive surgery, Macy told me. The Wolfes will make it happen.

But surgery means more pain.

I don't want any more pain.

Several stab wounds on my abdomen, and my front didn't take the worst of it.

Part of me is glad I can't see my back.

On my back are the whip marks. I was whipped a lot. They tried so hard to whip me into submission. One time, I got infected. Diamond brought in a physician that time, and I begged him to think about the Hippocratic oath he'd taken. To get us all out of there.

But whatever money he was paid meant more to him than his oath.

Still, he healed me. Gave me the antibiotics I needed to rid myself of the infection. And I got a three-week respite from the hunt.

The wounds healed.

Only to be open again. Again.

Again.

And again.

I have no more open wounds. A few aches and pains—reminiscent of what I've endured—but no worse than the aches and pains from being a professional athlete.

A professional athlete.

I actually made it onto a professional volleyball team after college.

If I hadn't?

I'd never have been taken to that damned island.

9

BUCK

I do it. I crash the minibar. I didn't drink at dinner. I didn't want to make Aspen uncomfortable. Now? I need a fucking shot of bourbon.

A couple tiny bottles of Jack sit in the door of the minifridge.

I grab one.

I grab another.

I open them and pour them into one of the lowball glasses on the table.

Then I shoot it. Jack isn't my favorite, but nothing stings quite as well as Tennessee corn mash whiskey.

Just what I need.

I can't get Aspen out of my mind. She's the most beautiful woman I've seen in a while, and it's funny, because she's not beautiful in the classic sense. She wears her dark hair short, in a pixie style, but she's so far from a pixie. She's tall and muscular with a strong body, slender hands with long fingers. Then her face... High cheekbones, full pink lips. Expressive dark eyes with long lashes.

Her bone structure…

Christ. When in hell have I *ever* considered a woman's bone structure?

Lovely breasts too. The perfect size. Probably around a C cup.

I like a good fuck as much the next guy. In fact, since I've been home from the last tour, fucking is all I've done with women. I haven't tried to start a relationship.

I don't expect that to change anytime soon.

Except…Aspen has me thinking about things.

Thinking about…the future. The future with a woman.

I figured I was too fucked up to even consider a future like that. My mother wants grandchildren, and I always said she'd get them from Emily and Johnny. But Johnny's a womanizer—a young stud who may never settle down. Emily is in a steady relationship now, but she's focused on her new position on Wolfe Island as an instructor at the art colony.

And her boyfriend, Scotty? He's a freaking beach bum. Oh, he loves Emily, and they will settle down and have children eventually, but not anytime soon.

The Jack was good, but it didn't hit the spot. I'm on edge, man, and the drab surroundings in this hotel room aren't helping. Five hundred bucks a night, and everything's beige? Even the print on the wall seems dull and colorless, with its brown and yellow tones.

Or maybe I'm drab and colorless. Or I should be, except that I can't get my attraction to Aspen Davis out of my mind.

I need to run a few laps, maybe take a swim.

I'm not swimming in a hotel pool. Hell, there might be families there. It's still early after all.

The gym then. I change into a T-shirt and shorts, and I

head down to the second floor where the workout room is located.

It's empty, thank God. I don't like working on the machines. I'd rather be outside, running in nature. I'm not a fan of weight machines either. I prefer free weights.

But weights aren't what I need right now. I need to work off some steam.

So as much as I hate it, I hit the treadmill. I program it for ten miles, uphill. Earbuds secured, and metallic rock blaring.

And I go. I fucking go. I succumb to my own energy as I listen to the head-banging music.

Good stuff.

The workout takes about forty-five minutes. Yeah, I do ten miles in forty-five minutes. One thing the Navy SEALs do is keep you in shape. For sure.

I grab a towel from the corner, wipe off my face and neck, and then I head back up to my room. I need a shower.

I feel better, my heart pounding and endorphins flowing through me.

But my leisure doesn't last long.

When I get to the door of my room, I hear the screams.

10

ASPEN

I'm drowning.

Each time I manage to get my head above water, I let out a shriek.

Then I'm underwater again. Something's holding me down.

No! Diamond says they can't kill us.

They can't drown me.

It won't happen.

But I can't, I can't, I can't... Can't hold my breath any longer.

I gasp in a breath above water once more, shriek, and I'm underwater again.

Sounds. Muffled sounds.

Fight. Fight back. Fight. It's all you have.

I break the grasp, bring my head above water, suck in some well-needed air.

The sounds. The pounding.

Where am I?

I stumble out of the water, reach a hard surface.

Naked. I'm naked. I scramble to my feet, ready to run.

From them.

Keep them from getting me.

The pounding. Pounding in my ears. Pounding around me. In my head, like a hammer sinking a nail into a two-by-four.

God, the pounding!

Nearly stumbling, I escape into a place that's...carpeted?

Pounding. Pounding. Pounding. I scream, covering my ears.

Aspen! Aspen! Open the door!

Aspen.

My name is Garnet. Who's Aspen?

Pounding. Pounding. Pounding. Against the door. Water drips from my body, and I...

I open the door.

And I remember.

Pictures hurl back to me. Images. Feelings.

I'm at the Four Seasons Hotel. And Buck. Good, strong Buck. He stands in front of me.

And I fall into his hard body.

"Easy, honey. Easy." He lifts me, takes me to the bed, and lays me down. Then he goes to the bathroom, brings back a towel, and wraps me in it.

Did he see the scars on my body? Did he see that I have only one nipple?

If he did, he didn't show it on his face. He showed no signs of being surprised. No signs of being disgusted.

He pushes my hair back off my forehead. "Okay. I'm here, honey. I'm here."

Tears squeeze out of my eyes.

Freaking tears. I never let myself cry on that damned island. I couldn't. Crying is weakness, and I couldn't be weak.

I had to be strong. I had to push back the pain, just like all those times on the volleyball court when I played with injuries because my team needed me.

I pushed through, and I pushed through on that island.

Now? In a soft and glorious bed in a five-star hotel, with the handsomest man in the universe taking care of me?

I can no longer push.

I sob. Soul-racking sobs. As if all the sobs I held inside during the last six years come tumbling out of me.

It's weak. *I'm* weak. I know this, but I can't bring myself to care enough to stop.

Okay, honey. I've got you. I've got you.

Buck's voice. Buck's strong, deep, masculine voice.

So comforting, and damned if I know why.

Being comforted by a man is not something I ever imagined. Not after what I've been through.

He sits on the bed next to me. He doesn't try to gather me in his arms, though part of me really wants him to.

The other part of me? That part wants to run screaming from him.

He doesn't force it. He just sits with me. At one point, he takes my hand, rubs his fingers in my palm, but then, as if he thinks better of it, he puts my hand down.

"I'm going to get you some clothes. You should be dry by now. I'll put you to bed. In my bed in my room. I'll sleep in here, on this wet stuff."

I open my mouth to tell him no, that's not necessary, but all that comes out is more sobbing.

Damn. I thought I was done.

But I cry and I cry.

I'm not sure I'll ever be done again.

He lets me cry.

He helps me sit up so I can blow my nose. Pats my back when I hiccup from the crying.

And then...I finally stop. No more tears. They just stop.

A few moments later, Buck rises, walks to the minibar, and comes back with a bottle of water. He opens it for me. "You need to drink this. You're dehydrated. From all the crying."

The word *crying* almost makes me start up again, but I choke it back. I take the water from him and drink half of it in the first sip.

"The rest," he says. "All of it."

Two more gulps and I drain the bottle.

"In half an hour I want you to drink another bottle. Okay?"

I nod. I'm not sure I trust myself to speak yet.

"I'm going to get you some pajamas. Are they in your bag?

I don't wear pajamas. I wear underwear and a T-shirt. But still, I say nothing. I'm still afraid to speak.

He gets into my suitcase, ravages through my belongings, and then rises. "I'll be back. I'm going to get you one of my T-shirts."

He returns with a large white T-shirt. Just a basic under-shirt. But it's huge, and even at six feet, I know it will hang on me.

He turns his head. "Put it on."

I can't. I just sit there, still wrapped in the towel.

"Aspen?"

"I'm fine."

The first words I've dared to speak. It's a lie. He and I both know that. All I need to do now is muster the strength to put on the T-shirt and then snuggle into his nice, warm bed while he sleeps here in my soaking one.

That's hardly fair.

But what the hell is fair about this life? Precious little from what I've seen.

I drop my towel just as he turns to meet my gaze.

His jaw drops. "I'm sorry."

For a moment I think he's going to turn around again, give me my privacy.

But instead— "Baby, I'm so, so sorry."

My scars.

He sees I have only one nipple. Only one nipple to feed a baby in the future, if I'm ever whole enough to be a mother.

Something that will always remind me.

Something that will always remind *him*.

Then I say the words. The words I need to say. The words I never thought I'd say again, and certainly not to a virtual stranger.

"I don't want to be alone tonight, Buck. I don't want to be alone."

11

BUCK

The marks on Aspen aren't anything I haven't seen before. I remember some Syrian refugees in Afghanistan who had been raped, beaten, mutilated by Taliban insurgents.

Most of them looked worse than Aspen looks now.

But my God...

This poor woman... What she's been through.

And in a way?

It's the most beautiful sight I've ever seen.

I want to touch her. I want to trace my fingers over every scar on her body, show her how beautiful she still is.

After all, I'm not without scars myself.

But what she's asking? I can't give it to her.

She's not asking for sex. She's asking not to be alone. I know the difference. She's not ready for sex. But if I let her lie with me, take her into my bed so she won't be alone...

I'm not sure I can leave her alone.

Okay, that's not true. I *can* control myself. I will be able to leave her alone.

But it will be one of the most difficult things I've ever done.

I've had to do a hell of a lot of difficult things in my life.

Not the least of which is bury four friends. Talk to their parents, their significant others.

Tell them how wonderful their sons, brothers, husbands were.

God, get over yourself, Buck.

Lying next to a beautiful woman and not touching her is not nearly as difficult as the things you've done in your life.

Just keep your fucking dick at bay for once. You can do it. You have to do it.

This woman needs you.

And you need to be there for her.

I walk toward her, take the T-shirt from her, and slide it over her head, help her poke her arms through the armholes. Then I lift her into my arms and carry her like a baby through the door leading to my room.

I lay her down on the bed and cover her. Then I walk to my minibar and grab another two bottles of water. I open them both and set one next to her on her nightstand. "When you're thirsty. It's right here."

She murmurs a thank you and shuts her red and swollen eyes.

I hate sleeping in a shirt. I always feel like I can't move, but the garment stays on, along with my workout shorts. I want Aspen comfortable.

I force myself to turn away from her, away from her scarred beauty, and away from her neediness.

But then...

Warmth envelops my back.

Aspen. Aspen is clinging to me.

Good God, give me strength.

"Aspen," I growl. "Don't."

"Please. Something about you. Something about you gives me...peace."

Peace? From me? I haven't felt peace in... Hell, I can't even remember.

But she needs me. And damn it, part of me—a very big part of me—needs her as well.

So I turn toward her, take her in my arms, and let her snuggle into my shoulder.

Already my groin is tightening, my dick is hard.

But I breathe in, out, in again. Keep myself in check. She smells like lavender—lavender and goodness and perfection.

All those scars on her beautiful body.

And still... Perfection.

I kiss the top of her head. Bury my nose in her fragrant short hair.

And then—

I groan.

Warm hands grip my cock.

"God, Aspen. Please. We can't."

"I need you. I have to go with that, Buck. I never thought I'd want this again. Not ever. Do you understand? Do you understand what I'm saying to you?"

I understand more than she knows.

I've been there.

I know what happened to those women on that island. The Wolfes gave me all the information. I needed all the information to do my job.

I also know all the horror I saw and experienced while I was deployed.

It's not all that different from what happened to Aspen.

Some of the things I never think about.

I've trained myself not to think about them. It's too humiliating, too degrading.

And yeah, I know everything. It wasn't my fault and all that bullshit. But wasn't it? Maybe... Maybe I just wasn't strong enough.

Maybe I took too many damned risks.

Too many damned risks when I should've been protecting my team. Protecting my friends.

And though I came home alive—strong and alive—there are things I could've prevented had I not taken stupid risks.

Rape. It doesn't happen only to women.

And it's no less dramatic.

Aspen needs a soft touch. A gentle touch. I'm not sure I have that in me.

But my God, her hand feels amazing around my cock. She's a large woman, and she has large hands. Large and strong hands.

Right now she's milking me like her life depends on it.

Knowing better, I reach toward her, touch her between her legs.

"Fuck, you're wet."

"I know," she murmurs. "I can't believe it either."

"An hour ago you were shrieking. Scared for your life. How...?"

"How indeed," she says. "How are you hard as a rock for me? How are you hard as a rock for a woman who was shrieking an hour ago, scared for dear life?"

She's right. There's no explanation for either of us. It makes absolutely zero sense.

"Please," she says again. "It doesn't mean anything. It doesn't have to mean anything. All I know is... I want this. I want you. I'm not talking about forever. I don't think I'll ever want forever with anyone. But right now, I want you. I want your body touching mine. Kissing mine. I know I'm a mess. I know I'm ugly."

"Ugly? My God. You're beautiful, Aspen."

"How can you say that? You've seen me. What they did to me."

"Easy." I sit up, turn on the light, and remove my T-shirt. "Look at me, Aspen. Take a moment, and just look at me."

12

ASPEN

He's beautiful. Muscular and beautiful and...his torso is full of scars. Perhaps even more scars than mine.

I reach forward, trace my fingers over each one. He's been cut. Multiple times. Shot.

"Turn around," I say.

"Why?"

"I want to see your back. You've seen mine."

He shudders a moment, I don't think he's going to grant my request when—

He turns.

What I see is both beautiful and horrible.

His back is also covered in scars. From whips, from knives.

It's also covered in tattoos.

Six individual images, and centered in the middle is a golden eagle clutching something. An anchor, maybe? And something that looks like a pitchfork. I cock my head. There's something familiar about it, but I can't quite remember...

Flames flare from the image, and the six designs around it are all about two inches in diameter.

My gaze drops to one in particular.

A buck.

A strong deer with branched antlers.

Buck.

I touch the buck, trace it with my fingers.

Then I trace the other images.

An eagle.

A phoenix rising from the ashes.

An ace of spades.

A ghost.

And a gorgeous gray wolf.

Something's different about four of them. The eagle, the ace, the ghost, and the wolf all have black halos over them.

I trail my fingers over each one again, and then over the scars that slash over and around and through them. He squirms against my caresses and clears his throat. "Sorry. It's just... You know..."

"I do," I say softly. "Tell me. Tell me what these all mean."

"The buck. He's me."

I kiss the buck tattoo on his back. "And the others?"

"The design in the middle is the Budweiser."

"You mean like the beer?"

"That's just a nickname because the acronym for some of the training we do is BUDS. I have it on my forearm as well." He shows me. "It's the Special Warfare Insignia or it's sometimes called the SEAL trident."

"A trident. That's what that thing is. All I could think of was a pitchfork."

"A Navy anchor, a trident, and a flintlock-style pistol. We

wear it when we complete all our training and are designated Navy SEALS."

"It's beautiful. Why the flames?"

He doesn't reply. Maybe there is no reason. Maybe there is, and he can't talk about it. Doesn't matter. I move to the ghost and trace it with my fingers.

"And the others? The other images?"

"My teammates. On my last tour, the Delta team. The phoenix is my friend who lived."

"And the others?" My throat catches.

"They didn't come back."

"The halos..." I trace the black ellipse over the wolf's head.

"Yes."

"My God," I say breathlessly. "I'm so sorry, Buck."

He turns then. Cups my cheek. "You don't have to be sorry. You've been through just as much if not more."

"But that doesn't negate everything you've been through. And your friends... I'm so very sorry."

"Aspen..."

I bring my head to his shoulder. "I didn't lose anyone. They weren't allowed to kill us. They could abuse us and torture us. Violate us in any way they wanted, but they couldn't kill us. They couldn't maim us. You didn't have that."

"No, I didn't. What I did have was a choice. I made the choice to join the Navy, to become a SEAL. I made the choice to serve my country."

"I know, but—"

"I made that choice, Aspen. You didn't make the choice. You didn't make the choice to go through what you went through."

He's right, of course. But it doesn't matter. Not in the end. We've both been through so much.

"Still... I'm sorry."

He pushes my head off his shoulder and meets my gaze. "I don't want you to be sorry."

"But I—"

"No. I don't want your sympathy. I don't want your pity. I don't want any of that. It only makes me feel worse."

"But why would it—"

"It just does." He touches my lips with his finger, igniting a tingle in me. "I don't know how to explain it any better than that. It just does."

I nod then. In a way, I get it. I don't particularly want sympathy or pity either. It makes me feel weaker.

It probably makes him feel weak as well.

But even looking at Buck, with all his scars, having lost four of his beloved friends, I see no sign of weakness.

There's not a weak bone in this man's body.

There never was, and there never will be.

I touch his cheek, let his rough black stubble scrape my fingertips. His lips are so beautiful. They're parted slightly, and I want so badly to kiss them.

He makes no move to kiss me. After all, he's not the one who wanted this. I am. I can't do this to him. Hell, I can't do it to myself. I'm not ready for it, and apparently neither is he.

I never imagined...

Sure, he said he did three tours in Afghanistan, but still, I never imagined that Buck might be the person who truly understands what I went through.

Even the other women on the island never understood. They didn't fight as hard as I did.

Except for Katelyn, who was treated nearly as badly as I

was when she was punished for stealing a ceramic plate—a ceramic plate that she didn't do anything with, that she had inflicted no harm with.

Still, they ambushed her, and she came back beaten and abused and tortured.

Diamond wasn't sure she'd make it.

But she did, and she became stronger after that.

All the women were strong. All of them fought back as much as they could. We were all "worthy prey," or we never would have been taken to that hell on earth.

But none of them fought as much as I did. The abusers were harder on me because of it, and even so, I couldn't stop fighting. It's not in me.

It's not in Buck either.

"I'm sorry," I tell him. "I'm sorry I came onto you like that. It's not a good idea. For either of us."

"No, it's not." His voice is gruff, needy, and full of yearning. "But I don't fucking care."

His mouth comes down on mine.

My lips are already parted, and his tongue sweeps between them. A kiss. A kiss from a man.

I was kissed on the island a few times, but for the most part, those degenerates weren't interested in kissing. They weren't interested in sex either. Sure, they fucked me, but it wasn't sex. It was a violation. It was rape, pure and simple.

Those men came to the island to hunt a strong woman. To use and abuse and torture a strong woman.

Maybe it made them feel better about themselves.

Buck Moreno? He doesn't need to abuse a strong woman to feel better about himself.

No. Strength exudes from him. It's a part of him as much as his heart or lungs or liver. No matter how scarred he is, no

matter what he's been through at his enemies' hands, he
exudes strength.

Even his kiss is strong. Passionate, full of longing, and
strong. He invades my mouth as if he's invading enemy
territory.

Only I'm far from an enemy, so I launch an invasion as
well—an invasion of Bucks mouth—and our tongues duel
and fight for control.

And my God... It's freaking amazing.

Magnificent. Two strong wills, and one deep passionate
and exciting kiss.

My nipple hardens, and my areola on my other breast
contracts. I feel what isn't there. The phantom nipple.

I never would've believed it.

I can feel my missing nipple.

The kiss becomes more raw, more feral, more full of pure
and unadulterated lust. It's so crushing in its intensity, and
my God, I never want it to stop. Our lips glide together, our
teeth clash, our tongues tangle.

Until he pulls away, breaking the kiss. "My God..."

I suck in some much-needed air, and then I turn toward
the nightstand where he left the bottle of water. I bring it to
my mouth, slurp half of it down my throat.

"Aspen," he growls.

"Buck."

"We shouldn't."

"I suppose not."

"But we're going to," he says. "We're going to, Aspen, so
unless you tell me now to go back to the other room, I'm
going to have you. Right here, in this bed. Tonight."

13

BUCK

With one hundred percent of my body and soul, I want her to say no. But I also want her to say yes.

The physical part of me—my dick and the rest of my throbbing body—needs to be with her. Needs to be inside her beautiful body. Needs to sate my desires, fulfill my needs with that beautiful athletic body of hers.

But the mental part of me? My brain? I know it's not a good idea. I know what she's been through, and I know I can't give her what she needs, which is a friend. A relationship.

I'm not ready for that. After what I've been through, I'm not sure I'll ever be wired that way again.

"Please," she says. "I want this. I need this. I have to have this now, because if I don't, I may never want it again. I may never have the chance. Not with you. Someone who makes me feel these things. And who makes me feel..."

"Makes you feel what?"

"Safe. You make me feel so safe, Buck."

Safe.

Damn. She said the one thing that makes me want her even more. All these years, I've berated myself. I've hated myself for taking risks instead of keeping my teammates safe like I should have.

Sure, I did some amazing heroic things for my country. But my friends—my blood brothers—died. If I'd been paying better attention to them, perhaps I could have saved them.

But here's this woman—this strong woman who's been through so much—telling me that I make her feel safe.

It guts me. It totally guts me.

I plunder her mouth once more. I kiss her in a way I've never kissed a woman. It's not just a kiss. It's a taking—a taking of what she's offering.

And I know it's not going to end with a kiss.

All she's wearing is my T-shirt and a pair of panties. I'm wearing workout shorts. That's all that stands between her body and mine.

Her beautiful, scarred body.

Even if it were perfection—with no scars—it couldn't be more beautiful to me.

In a way, we probably get each other more than anyone else would.

I want to protect her. I want to protect her the way I couldn't protect my buddies.

I want to take all my guilt and resentment and feeling of powerlessness, hide it away in my head, and shove myself into her body. Take from her what I need and give to her what she desires.

She deserves better than me, but she wants me, and I want her.

Such a powerful kiss. I enjoy kissing, I always have, but never did I imagine it could be like this.

This kiss is almost like a fuck.

It's so intense.

She opens for me so completely. She knows she's not ready. I know I'm not ready. And maybe that makes it even better. Maybe that makes it even more necessary.

It's unreal how much I want her and how I feel the same from her.

Her fingers are inside my shorts again, around my cock again. I can barely take it. I don't want a hand job from her, but if I don't stop this now, lead her where I want her, I'm going to explode just from her stimulation.

Manual stimulation.

I break the kiss, and I'm struck with a feeling of pure loss when her lips leave mine.

"Aspen..."

"Please," is all she says.

She's wet. I already know this. I slide my hand beneath the waistband of her panties, and she wriggles out of them.

Then her shirt—

"No," she says. "It's your shirt. I like it. It makes me feel...safe."

"Please. You're so beautiful."

"I'm not. Not anymore."

"You are to me."

I leave her shirt though. I want her to feel comfortable. Safe. I slide out of my boxers, and though I want to kiss her whole body, what she needs—and what I need—is a coupling. A joining.

So I slide inside her, and God, she's slick and wet and so fucking ready.

Fulfillment. Fulfillment like I've never felt before. A groan leaves my throat just as a soft sigh escapes Aspen's lips.

"Yes," she sighs. "God, yes."

"Good?"

"So good." She bites her bottom lip. "Never imagined I could feel this again."

I understand what she means. I want to say so, but the words don't come. My entire world has become my cock, and all I want to do is stay here, balls deep, enjoying the suction of her pussy around me.

A moment later, though, my body rebels. I pull out and push back in, letting her friction glove me, milk me.

Even I'm surprised at how ready I am, as my balls scrunch close to my body, ready to shoot into her.

Will she come? I don't know, but I want her to. I want to make her feel as good as she's making me feel.

I lean down and kiss her lips softly. I trail over her pretty face to her earlobe where I nibble gently and then shove my tongue into her ear.

She moans beneath me, wrapping her long legs around my waist.

And then I can't go slowly anymore. I plunge into her and explode.

She moans beneath me. Clearly she's enjoying herself, even though I know she hasn't had an orgasm. How could she? I haven't touched her clit. I haven't kissed her body.

All I've done is focus on my own selfish pleasure.

I stay embedded inside her for a few precious seconds, but then I roll off her and lie on my back.

"Thank you," she says.

Thanking me? Really? "You deserved better than that," I say.

"That was exactly what I needed. I just needed to feel you inside me. I needed to feel safe."

"But you didn't—"

"I don't care. That's not what I was after, Buck."

"But—"

"Women are different. Surely you know that."

"Of course I do. But still... A climax feels damned good."

"It does. But I don't care about that, at least not tonight. I needed to feel you inside me. I needed to feel safe, comforted. And that's what you gave me."

"I don't understand. How can you...? After everything...?"

"Believe me, it's a puzzle to me as well. But it's what I needed, what I wanted, and you gave it to me." She smiles. "You know what?"

"What?"

"I think I may be able to sleep tonight. With you next to me. I never thought it would be possible."

"I'll go to the other room."

"Why would you say that? After I just said I may sleep tonight with you here?"

I say nothing then. She's right.

But the truth is? I don't want to sleep with her tonight.

Because quite frankly, she got what she wanted. She's done.

But I am not. And being here? With her right next to me?

It might be more than I can take. I'll leave her alone. I'm not that guy. But damn, I'm already getting hard again.

14

ASPEN

What is it about this man?

Sometimes, I remember things from my past. Like the first time Brandon and I slept together, spent the night in each other's arms.

I wasn't overly experienced, and I didn't have an orgasm. But I enjoyed myself. It wasn't until later that I had an orgasm with him, and after that, sex without an orgasm was always a disappointment for me.

Tonight? Tonight was not a disappointment at all. It's been a long time since this body felt an orgasm, and if it never has another, I'm not sure I care.

I'm not looking for that physical pleasure. I'm looking for comfort. For safety. For someone to protect me.

And this man—Buck—he did all of that and more.

So much more.

His body is as scarred as my own.

Those tattoos... Those halos...

There were times on the island—times when a woman

wouldn't come back. Ruby. Turquoise. Both were there when I arrived. Then one day? They didn't return.

Ruby disappeared first. Diamond, of course, wouldn't tell us what happened. Did she even know? She was our house mother, an older woman who, though it was clear she had once been beautiful, had turned into a shadow of her former self.

I don't know her story, why she was there. In her way, she cared. Even loved us, I think.

There was always a look of sadness in her eyes. Especially when one of us was hurt—I mean truly *physically* hurt.

The other kind of hurt? That never went away. Ruby was one of the most beautiful women on the island, with dark—nearly black—hair and brown eyes. She was called Ruby because of her naturally red lips. She had the kind of lips I would've been envious of had I been back in the real world. On the island? Not so much. Her lips got her attention I didn't want.

Too much attention, because one day she never came back.

I asked Diamond if Ruby had escaped. Diamond didn't reply, but her eyes looked sunken, sad, clouded. Far away.

Her eyes told the truth. Ruby hadn't escaped the island. No one could escape the island.

Ruby died. I don't know how. The men weren't allowed to kill us, but a lot of them came close. I was laid up more than once from injuries, taken off the hunt until I healed.

In a way, I rejoiced in physical injury. It gave me a respite from the horror of the daily life.

Turquoise was also beautiful. All the women on the island were. That's why we were taken in the first place.

I grew to hate my beauty. I grew to hate my athletic body,

even though it was my strength and endurance that helped me.

When you're an athlete—anywhere from the high school level on—you're taught to push yourself to the limits, to the point where you're ready to crash and burn, and then force yourself to find just a little bit more. Go deep inside yourself and grit your teeth and power through.

It was that attitude that helped me survive life on that island.

And it's that attitude that will keep me going now.

I think about Ruby and Turquoise when I envision Buck's tattoo—the friends he lost.

Ruby and Turquoise weren't really my friends. None of us were friends on that island. We were just trying to survive, and we talked from time to time, but most of us were quiet in the dorm. Moonstone, Onyx, and I sometimes watched TV together in the great room. The set played only old black-and-white sitcoms—*I Love Lucy, Leave it to Beaver, Father Knows Best*.

In fact, I was with Onyx and Moonstone when we were rescued—when Rock and Reid Wolfe came to the island, and Diamond...

What happened to Diamond?

No one seems to know. I've asked around.

Maybe Buck knows.

He's lying next to me, his eyes closed, but he's not asleep. I can tell. He's trying to sleep, but something's bothering him.

Does he have nightmares too? Does he have nightmares about those angels on his back? About what he went through? About the times those scars were branded onto his body?

How could he not?

Oh, the thoughts... The blurred thoughts that plague me, steal my sleep from me. And once I do find sleep, the nightmares...

So much I don't remember. So much I've blocked from my mind. I have to face it all. I have to face it all if I want to heal.

And lying next to Buck? My head in the crook of his shoulder, as I breathe in his warm and masculine scent?

I almost want to.

I almost want the memories to return, so I can heal fully.

I JERK UPWARD IN BED, covering my ears over the noise.

The shrieking, God, the shrieking...

Then someone shaking me. Gripping my shoulders.

And I realize...

The shrieking is coming from *me*.

"Aspen. Aspen, wake up. It's okay."

The voice. The deep and comforting voice.

I recognize it, but the eyes staring at me? I don't recognize them at all.

My throat is raw. Raw and hurting and burning. And I'm still screaming, screaming, screaming...

"Aspen. Baby, it's me. It's Buck."

Buck...

Buck...

The howling shrieks. Again, again, again...

"Aspen... Please... Baby..."

Buck. Buck.

Beautiful, muscular Buck. Buck, who keeps me safe.

The last shriek is softer, and it leaves me with a scratchy throat.

Then strong arms are around me, strong fingers massaging my back, soft whispers in my ear.

"It's okay, baby. It's okay. I'm here."

I grab onto him, hold on for dear life.

"It's okay. You were having a nightmare. It's okay. Breathe, baby. Breathe.

His hardness. His strength. His calm and deep voice. It's all like a lighthouse on the darkest night. A beacon. A beacon with a heartbeat.

I find I *can* breathe. In, out, and in again.

My heartbeat hammers against my sternum, but still I breathe. In. Out. In. Out. Again. Again.

Buck's lips against the top of my head. His strong heartbeat that overshadows my own. His warm skin, his hard, taut muscles.

Enveloping me. Enveloping all of me. Warming me and soothing me, like a comforting salve.

Then—

"Aspen, baby. What have we gotten ourselves into?"

15

BUCK

I swear to God my heart is pounding as quickly as hers is. When I woke up to her shrieking, I was back in the foxhole. Saving my own damned skin instead of someone else's.

Never again.

My poor baby.

But she's not my baby. I barely know her. Yet I feel closer to her than I've felt to anyone in a long time.

She's clamped onto me, only my large T-shirt between us.

I kiss the top of her head again and stroke her soft hair.

"It's okay, baby. You're okay."

She's quiet now, still clamped against me, but then I feel her movement. Her fingers trailing up my back, and though she can't see what she's doing and neither can I, I know she's tracing the images of my fallen friends.

I'm not sure how long we lie there clinched together. I know only that I'm relaxed now. Relaxed with this woman clinging to me for safety.

The thought is frightening. Frightening and yet so consuming.

"Try to sleep," I say softly.

She doesn't reply, just closes her eyes, still snuggled up to me.

Nightmares. My old friends—except not my friends. No more nightmares for Aspen. Not on my watch. I need to protect this woman.

And I can. I will. I will protect her physically.

But what's going on in her head? I can't protect her from that, no matter how much I wish to.

It's a few hours later before I finally fall asleep.

I OPEN my eyes and stretch.

Then I jerk upward.

"Aspen? Where are you?"

I rise, wrap a sheet around my waist, and head into her adjoining room. From there I hear the whoosh of the shower.

Part of me—a very hard part of me—wants to join her in the shower. Sure, we engaged in the act last night. We were as close as two people can be.

But we know so little about each other. We've both been through so much. So I can't. I can't join her in the shower no matter how much my body is commanding me to.

Instead, I head to my own shower, and as much as I hate cold showers, I need one. I need to get rid of this constant hard-on. It's not helping either of us.

Today is big for Aspen. She's going to see her old boyfriend. Her parents. Whoever she wants to. I'll either go with her or I won't. Scratch that. I *will* go with her. I just may sit outside in the car while she does her thing. It's her call.

My sources came through with an address for Brandon Page. Turns out he's still unmarried, which bugs me more than it should. But that doesn't mean Aspen wants him or that he still wants her. In his mind, she disappeared five years ago.

Most likely he's moved on.

Damn. I hope he's moved on.

But who am I to say? Whoever this Brandon is, he was willing to put a ring on her finger, and she accepted.

All I know is that she wants to speak to him. I don't know what about. But surely... If she wants him back...she wouldn't have let me fuck her last night.

Then again, she's messed up. As messed up as I am. Who the hell knows why she let it happen? Who the hell knows why *I* let it happen?

Except I do know. Something about her cried out to me. I had to have her, and of course it didn't help that she was begging me.

Damn.

I close my eyes, inhale the steam from the shower, and realize I neglected to set the faucets on cold.

It's okay though. The steam fogs up the mirror, and I close my eyes.

And then I'm back.

Back in the damned foxhole.

～

"QUIET!" *I whisper harshly to Ghost.*

Ghost is just a kid. He's straight out of seal training, with red hair and freckles and skin so fair we call him Ghost. I've tried to take him under my wing, and so has Phoenix.

But Ghost is determined to make it on his own, and I have to hand it to him: he's more disciplined than I was at his age.

Right now? All I want him to do is shut the fuck up.

He got his elbow shot. The elbow.... Fuck man, elbow pain is harsh. Bone fragments speckle the wound.

Pain. God, the pain he must be enduring. Would I be able to contain my screams in his place?

Doesn't matter. Insurgents are right above us, and if he doesn't shut the fuck up, they'll find us for sure.

I have no choice. I pull out my switchblade and hold it against the pale flesh of his neck.

"You shut up, or I swear to God I'll slit your fucking throat."

He gasps in a breath, holds it.

The blade scratches his flesh, and a bubble of blood rises.

Ghost chokes back another scream.

My God, the pain he must be enduring.

I know that kind of pain. I know how hard it is not to scream. I've been electrocuted, sliced open, sodomized...

And all those times, I screamed like someone was cutting off a limb. Like a fucking pussy.

Would I have been able to stay quiet if someone had held a blade to my neck?

I don't know. The degenerates got off on my screams.

Maybe I should've held back. If I had, maybe they would've tortured me less.

None of that matters now. Because if those insurgents find us in this damned foxhole, we're both dead.

Ghost is bleeding out. He's going to die eventually. If I slit his throat, I might be doing him a favor. He'll simply die quicker, and he won't have to worry about not screaming anymore.

But I can't do it. Can't bring myself to fucking kill the kid.

I like Ghost. He had a lot of potential, but then he had to go get his elbow shot off.

He ran. Adrenaline stayed with him, and he ran with me until I dragged him into this hiding place.

Now here we are. My adrenaline is still high because of my survival instinct. Both our lives could be over in a matter of seconds.

But Ghost? Once he got down here, he succumbed to the pain.

I want to comfort him. Tell him I've got him. But I can't. I can't show him any warmth, any friendship, any love.

I have to keep him scared. I have to keep him quiet. And for that, I need my damned switchblade at his neck.

Again I argue inside myself. Would I be doing him a favor if I ended it all now? Leave him pain-free?

No... There's always a chance. Still a fucking chance we can get out of this.

I've gotten out of worse scrapes.

Much worse scrapes, where I was being tortured, abused. They shaved my head. They shaved my genitals. They whipped my back and my legs. They fucking raped me with a broom handle.

But I survived. I escaped.

And damn it all to hell, I will escape this time too.

Ghost is a liability. If I end it now, my chances are better alone.

But I can't.

I can't kill a friend.

His breath sounds are weak, shallow, but I don't move the blade. I can't fucking move the blade.

He gasps. Opens his mouth.

"Buck..."

His last word.

With one last gasp between his blue lips, he leaves his body.

He's gone.

I keep hold of the switchblade, and I wait. I wait, knowing they may come and drag me out of here any minute.

And for that minute, I don't care.

I can think only about how I threatened my friend—my brave, young friend.

And he ended up dying anyway.

16

ASPEN

I almost hate to shower. I don't want to wash the smell of Buck off me.

Even now I can't believe I'm having these thoughts. All those times on the island, when I couldn't wait to clean the filth of those men from me.

Even now, it feels all wrong—what I let Buck do to me.

It feels right at the same time. So right that I don't ever want it to end.

But it will. Buck won't stay with me forever. Only until I'm safely back in Manhattan at my apartment.

And today...

Today I have to see Brandon.

I have to tell him that I didn't leave him intentionally. That I didn't—

I close my eyes, tilt my face upward, and let the warm water rain over me.

Brandon...

Once I thought he was the one. How different my life would be if I hadn't been taken.

I'd probably still be playing volleyball, but as I got older, my career would be coming to an end. I'd be married, and maybe Brandon and I would be thinking about a family once I stopped playing professionally. I'd get a coaching job.

Those were our plans—the plans we always talked about.

Then I disappeared.

No body was found, and my family and friends—and Brandon—moved on. They had to. I'd have done the same thing. Survival depends on it.

I turn off the water, step out of the shower, and wrap myself in a white bath sheet. I use another towel to dry off my hair. It's so short that I don't need to do much to it.

I cut it off as soon as I got to the retreat center on the island. I'll never wear it long again. It's just something more that the men were able to grab. To bring me down.

They never shaved me. Katelyn told me once that they shaved her head before she came to the island, while she was still being held captive in...that concrete place. I don't know where it was.

Katelyn was on the island when I got there. She spent nearly ten years there.

Ten fucking years.

What's going on with her? She went to LA because her father was having some kind of surgery. I should call her. I have her number. I'll ask Buck. Maybe, after we leave Colorado, we can go see her in LA.

Then I smile as something hits me. I'm trying to extend this time. Extend this time with Buck. I don't want it to end.

That's something. It's something because it's not a negative feeling, and I haven't had any feelings except negative ones for so long.

The Wolfes gave me pocket money, and I bought some

clothes while I was in Manhattan. I grab what I need out of my carry-on and dress in skinny jeans and a black T-shirt and flip flops. This is how I used to dress, and it feels normal to me even after everything.

I'm putting stuff in my purse when Buck peeks through the adjoining door. "Feel like breakfast?"

Oddly, I do. I actually feel like eating this morning.

"Sure."

"There's a buffet downstairs, or we can go somewhere else."

"The hotel buffet is fine. This is The Four Seasons, after all."

"True enough. Anytime you're ready."

I zip my purse closed. "How about now?"

"Absolutely."

Buck looks amazing. He's wearing jeans—the same ones as yesterday. I guess he didn't bring a suitcase. His military boots, and a plain white T-shirt. And damn, I can see every group of muscles on his torso through that thin cotton.

He's freshly showered, his hair damp.

"You doing okay?" he asks.

"Yeah. I'm sorry about my nightmare."

"Hey." He trails a finger over my cheek. "You don't ever need to apologize to me. About anything. You hear me?"

I tingle at his touch as I nod.

He smiles. "I mean it."

"I understand."

"After what you've been through, Aspen, you don't need to apologize to anyone."

I lift my eyebrows.

"Did I say something wrong?"

"No. Not all. I've been trying to figure out what I'm going

say to Brandon when I see him, and of course my first inclination is to apologize. But you're right. I didn't do anything. Not intentionally. I don't owe him an apology."

"No, you don't. But maybe he owes you one."

"Why would he owe me one?"

"We don't know if he does. Did he do anything to try to find you? Did your parents? I just don't know."

"I don't know either. Like I said, I haven't seen my parents. I've hardly spoken to them."

"I'm sure they tried to find you."

"I'm sure they did. I'm an only child, as you know. They adored me. It must have nearly killed them to lose me."

"Hey, they haven't lost you."

"No. Except they kind of have. I'm not the same woman I was. I don't think I ever will be."

"People change, Aspen."

I get what he's saying. I do. But he also gets what *I'm* saying. I may have changed in five years no matter what, but after five years in captivity? Five years of being hunted like an animal? Of being tortured, abused, raped?

That changed me in ways they'll never be able to understand.

We head downstairs and grab breakfast at the buffet.

Again, I'm surprised that I feel like eating. I fill my plate with some scrambled eggs, two slices of bacon, and a cinnamon Danish while Buck stands in the omelet line.

I head back to our table, and the server brings me the coffee and orange juice I ordered.

I mumble a quick thank you.

The eggs taste good. So does the bacon, but the Danish is kind of dry. Maybe I just got a bad one. This is still The Four Seasons, after all.

Buck rejoins me and digs into his omelet.

"How is everything?" he asks.

"Fine."

"It's good to see you eating. You only ate half of your meal last night."

"I wasn't hungry.

He smiles then, his whole face lights up. "I guess you worked up an appetite between then and now."

Warmth flows to my cheeks. I didn't do anything. I lay there. But it was perfect. So perfect and exactly what I wanted and needed.

"Aspen?"

I swallow my bite of eggs. "Yes?"

"I want you to know something. Last night... It meant something to me."

"It meant something to me too."

"I mean... It wasn't just a fuck to me."

"To me either."

He wrinkles his forehead. He's trying to say something, but he doesn't quite know how to say it. I get it.

"I don't want you to think I was using you," I say. "I mean, I suppose in a way I was. You make me feel safe, and that's what I was after. But it was more than that for me too. I wasn't using you, Buck."

"I know you weren't. I wasn't using you either."

I smile then, take a sip of coffee.

"You've been through so much," he says. "I don't want to push you."

"You didn't."

"No, but thank you for saying that." He smiles again. "It took every ounce of strength I possessed not to join you in the shower this morning."

Warmth tingles through me. I open my mouth to speak but no words emerge.

"You don't have to say anything," he says.

"It's just that I'm not sure what to say. Part of me really likes that idea, but..."

"And that's the reason I didn't do it," he says. "Because last night was something special. Something unique that may not happen again."

"You mean... You don't want it to happen again?"

"God, that's not what I said at all. It's sure as hell not what I meant." He rubs his forehead.

A slight smile curves onto my lips. "It meant something to me. It meant so much to me. And Buck... I don't think I'm ready for it to be over."

"Good. I'm not ready for it to be over either."

"I'm not saying I want to... You know..."

"What? Have some kind of big relationship?"

"Right. I mean, maybe eventually."

"I think we're both in similar places, baby."

"I've seen your scars, Buck. You may be right."

His gaze falls to the table, to his nearly empty plate. "Don't compare yourself to me. And don't underestimate what you've been through, Aspen. No one should be put through what you went through. Sure, I've been through some shit as well, but not for five years straight. I had pockets of abuse and torture, but not five years of it."

I look down at my plate and play with the remaining eggs, moving them around with my fork.

"I didn't mean to upset you," he says.

"You didn't. I just don't like to think about it. There's so much I don't remember, so much I don't *want* to remember. That's why I can't be in a relationship either. Not until I get to the point where I'm ready to face what happened to me. That's the only way I can fully heal, according to the therapists."

"If you have a lot more healing to do, I'm surprised you're not still at the retreat center."

"I left against medical advice," I say. "They wanted me to stay. It was a safe place where I could do my healing without any threat, but I had to leave the island. I just had to."

"I understand. More than you know."

"Like leaving Afghanistan. For you, I mean."

"Yeah. I think it probably was."

I drop my gaze to my plate again.

We don't say anything else for the rest of breakfast.

17

BUCK

"You should call him first," I say.

Aspen shakes her head. "No. I have to see him. I have to talk to him. Calling him gives him a chance to say no."

"Aspen..."

"No," she says again. "It's better to rip the bandage off."

I open my mouth to argue, but then I think better of it. I stop fighting her. Reid told me she gets whatever she wants or needs. If this is what she wants, even if I think it may be a bad idea, I have to go with it, and I will be there to protect her every step of the way.

Brandon lives in a northern suburb of Denver called Westminster. As far as I could find out, he's not married, but that doesn't mean he's single. I have an address and a phone number, and the address of his employer—a local news service where he works as a reporter.

We arrive at his townhome at ten a.m. It's a nice looking place with a lot of greenery surrounding what appears to be a man-made lake. Mallard ducks and Canada geese swim in the water and waddle around the neighborhood.

Aspen and I sit in the car for a moment.

"I don't know what to do," she says.

"I'll go with you. Or we can turn around and drive out of here. Whatever you want."

"No, I have to see him.

"I understand."

That's not a lie. I do understand. There were people I needed to see when I returned to the States, especially that last time— the time when I had to talk to the families of my fallen friends. Things didn't go as well as I wanted them to in some instances. And I'm afraid... I'm afraid that will happen to Aspen as well.

Finally, she sucks in a deep breath. "I'm ready."

I move to get out of the car.

"No. I have to do this alone."

"Are you sure?"

She clicks open the car door, hesitates a moment, and then opens it. "I'm sure."

I touch her left wrist. "Wait a minute."

She turns to me, her eyebrows raised.

"Pull my number up on your phone. Right now. Do it."

"Okay."

"That way you can reach me in an instant. All right? You hear me?"

"Buck, this man isn't dangerous."

"I'm sure he's not." Although honestly, I don't know at all. "But if anything happens, if you're even slightly uncomfortable, or if..."

"If...I have some kind of flashback or something?"

"Anything, Aspen. Please, baby. Do this for me."

She smiles then—sort of, anyway—pulls my number up on her phone, and shows me the screen. "Okay?"

I nod, and she leaves the car.

I'm parked on the street, and I watch her as she walks up the pathway. Brandon lives in a corner unit. His parking must be in the back somewhere.

She reaches the door, and then she hesitates. She brings her hand up, ready to knock, puts it down again, brings it back up.

I'm about ready to leave the car, to go get her, when—

She knocks on the door.

Is there a doorbell? I have no idea. I can't see closely enough from here. But maybe she's knocking for a reason. Maybe she just wants to pound something. I get it.

When no one comes to the door, she knocks again.

Again, I'm ready to spring to action when—

The door opens.

It's a woman.

I have no idea what Aspen says. I can't hear.

But then Aspen walks into the townhome and the door closes.

18

ASPEN

"I'll get him. Come on in."

The woman wears a pink lounging outfit. Probably her pajamas. It's after ten, but it *is* Saturday, after all. It never occurred to me that I might be waking Brandon up.

She's beautiful—auburn hair, rosy cheeks, no makeup. Is this how she looks when she gets out of bed? I look like a wet dishrag when I get out of bed.

"Bran!" She yells up the stairs. "There's someone here to see you."

Bran? He used to hate it when I called him that. "I'm not fiber," he would say.

"Be right down!"

Brandon's voice. I wondered if I'd recognize it. It's the same. Exactly the same.

I watch the stairs until he appears. He's wearing jeans and a plain white T-shirt, no shoes, his hair a mass of curls.

I wait for my body to react, to show me I still feel something for this man.

When he sees me, he squints, and then his eyes pop into circles. He stumbles down the rest of the stairs, sounding like a stampede of wildebeests.

"Aspen? Is it really you?"

He looks at me then. Stares at me. Nearly loses his footing as he takes the last step from the staircase.

"Bran?" the woman says. "Who is this?"

"Oh my God. Aspen. It *is* you."

"I'm waiting here," the other woman says.

"Oh my God. Charity, I'm sorry. This is Aspen. She..."

"It's a long story, Brandon," I say.

"I heard rumors. Rumors about... That you might be alive... I was going to call your parents, but..." He glances at the other woman—Charity.

"Wait. What?" Charity looks from me to Brandon to me again.

"This is Charity. She's my..."

"Girlfriend?" I say. "Fiancée?"

"Significant other is what we say," Charity offers.

"It's nice to meet you." I hold out my hand.

I'm shaking. I don't realize it until I try to shake Charity's hand.

She doesn't offer me hers. Instead—

"Anyone want to clue me in here?" she says.

"My God... You look... You look the same," Brandon says. "Except your hair. It's... I like it short."

His words are lost on me. I absolutely *don't* look the same. But again, they didn't mess with my face on the island. If he saw me naked, he'd see the truth.

But apparently that will never happen. Not with Charity here.

It's not that I want Brandon back. And I certainly didn't

expect him to wait five years for me, especially when he may have thought I skipped town and left him.

In fact, now that I look at Brandon, I'm not sure how I was ever attracted to him. He's slightly shorter than I am, but a lot of men are. He's still as good looking as he ever was—unruly blondish hair, blue eyes. A nice masculine jawline. Decent body.

God, though, he's nothing compared to Buck Moreno.

"Can we sit down?" I ask.

"Sure. Is there coffee, Charity?"

"Yeah. I'll get you both a cup. How do you take yours?" she asks me.

"Just black."

"Got it."

Charity disappears into the small kitchen, and Brandon takes my hand, leading me to the couch. He directs me to sit down, and then he sits next to me.

"My God."

"I just want you to know," I say. "I didn't leave you."

"I never thought that. God, Aspen, we all thought you were dead."

"I wasn't. I've been through..." I shake my head. "I don't want to go into it. It's hard to talk about. But I'm back. I'm okay. I'm alive."

"Did you... I mean, did you come here to..."

"No, Brandon. I never expected you to wait around for me. Charity seems like a nice person."

"She is. She's lovely, but she's not you. She never was."

Goodness. Is he actually holding a torch for me after all these years? "I'm not *me* anymore, Brandon."

I'm Garnet.

The words almost escape my lips. I'm *not* Garnet. I never

was. But Garnet is a part of me now, a part of me that will always be there.

Charity returns with our coffee. "I'll leave you two alone."

"It's okay," I say. "This is your house."

"Actually, Charity," Brandon says, "if you don't mind..."

She nods and heads back up the stairs.

"She could've stayed," I say.

"No. I don't want her to hear what I have to say to you."

My heart begins to beat rapidly. Surely he's not...

"I've missed you so much," he says. "Part of me can't believe my eyes. I thought I was over you, but now... Seeing you here..."

I bite my lower lip. This can't be happening. "Brandon, I didn't come here to get back together."

"Of course. I know that. I just... I love Charity. I really do."

Charity is much more beautiful than I ever was, but I don't say this. Plus she's about five eight, which works with Brandon's five eleven.

"How long have you been together?" I ask.

"About a year now. She moved in a couple months ago."

"So this is your place? You own it?"

"Yeah. I've been here for a few years."

"Still reporting?"

"Yeah. It doesn't pay too much, but it leaves me plenty of time to work on my writing."

"What does Charity do?"

"She's between jobs at the moment."

"Oh?"

"Yeah. She's a model."

"Really? She's beautiful, but..."

"She's not tall like you. I know. Though five nine is still tall for a woman."

"I suppose. I judged her to be about five eight looking at her. I guess I was a little off."

Silence for a moment. Then—

"Well... I guess I'll go."

"Don't you want your coffee?"

"No, not really. I've got someone waiting for me outside in the car."

Brandon grabs my arm. "Aspen, no. You can't just turn back up in my life right now and leave. I need to know. I need to know what went on. That you're all right."

I nudge my arm away. His touch feels all wrong.

"I'm fine, Brandon."

"Can't we... Can we get to know each other again?"

"I'm not sure how Charity would feel about that."

"Charity is..." He glances toward the stairs.

"She's what?"

He lowers his voice. "She's beautiful, and sweet, and lovely... But she isn't you."

"I told you already. I'm not *me* anymore." I rise, walk toward the door.

But Brandon pulls on my arm—

And I let out a shriek.

19

BUCK

I didn't stay in the car. I couldn't. I'm standing at the door, and—

A blood freezing shriek. From Aspen.

I grab the doorknob, twist it, and the door opens. I race in. A man is holding Aspen's left arm.

"Get your fucking hands off of her!"

A woman dressed in pink comes running down the stairs—

At the exact same moment my fist makes contact with the man's—I'm guessing Brandon's—face.

The woman in pink rushes to the man, who's now on the floor.

I grab Aspen and grip her shoulders. "Baby, are you all right?"

"Buck... What are you..."

"I heard you scream. He had his hands on you."

"He... It's okay..."

The woman next to Brandon looks up at me. "This is our home. What do you think you're doing?"

"I'm protecting her. She screamed." I shake my head. "I don't have to explain myself to you or anyone."

Aspen touches my cheek then. A soft and gentle touch, which I don't deserve.

"You do have to explain yourself to *me*," she says softly.

How do I explain? She screamed, and I acted on instinct.

"I heard you. Your scream. It was a reaction."

"I didn't mean to scream, Buck. I was leaving, and he grabbed my arm."

"Why? Why the hell did you grab her arm?"

"I wasn't done talking to her," Brandon says from the floor.

"You shouldn't have put your hands on her."

"Buck, it's okay. He didn't know."

"Know what?" the woman asks.

"Buck, please... I don't want to get into it."

I wrap my arms around Aspen. "Let's go."

"I think that's best," the woman says.

"It was nice to meet you, Charity," Aspen says.

"Aspen, wait..." From Brandon on the floor.

"I have nothing more to say," Aspen says.

"You heard the lady," I say gruffly.

"But... I just want to know you're okay. I want to know..."

"You want to know what?" Charity says, indignantly.

"I'm sorry," Brandon says. "I love her. I've always loved her."

Charity's jaw drops.

My jaw drops.

Aspen's jaw drops.

And something else consumes me. Like a thousand knives poking into me all at once.

I want to pummel the man on the floor. Pummel him into the dirt. Because no way is he going to take this woman.

"Aspen..." From Brandon again.

"I'm sorry, Brandon. I need to leave."

Charity rises. "Apparently I need to leave as well."

"No, Charity..." Again from Brandon.

"I'm sorry, Brandon. I always felt like you weren't giving me a hundred percent. Now I know why. You've been pining away for your first love."

"I thought she was dead."

"I *am* dead," Aspen says. "The person you knew, Brandon —she's dead."

"No. Please..."

"Let's go, Buck," Aspen says. "You were right. I should've called him."

I'm not going to say I told her so. But honestly, I don't think either of us expected that this man would still be in love with Aspen.

I mean, come on, he's got this gorgeous piece of woman in pink.

But as beautiful as she is—and she *is* beautiful—she's nothing compared to Aspen.

Aspen, whose eyes can look into a person's soul. Whose lips are like the finest silk.

And whose pussy gloves my cock like no one else's.

I'm jealous already. This man has probably felt Aspen's pussy, has probably tasted it. Something I haven't done.

Something I'm going to do.

"We're out of here," I say.

"Aspen, no! Please!"

I lead her out the door and close it behind us. Then I meet her gaze. "Are you okay?"

"No, Buck. I'm so far from okay." She falls into my arms.

I pick her up and carry her to the car like a child.

"You'll be okay," I tell her, once she's securely in the car. "I give you my word, as a man of honor. I will make sure you're okay."

We drive back to the hotel in silence. She was going to see her parents today, but already I can tell she's not up to that. Once we're back in her room, I sit next to her on the bed.

"Tell me," I say.

"I had no idea, Buck."

"I know. Believe me, I would've thought he moved on by now."

"Apparently he thought he did. And now... Poor Charity."

"She'll be fine. He doesn't deserve her anyway, if he was in love with someone else all this time."

"It's strange," she says. "All this time, and I got over him. I mean, I didn't really have a choice. I was thrown into horror, and my emotions became a hindrance."

God, I get what she's saying. I so get it.

"I never imagined he still loved me all this time."

Who couldn't love Aspen? I can see Brandon's dilemma. I see it very clearly.

"Buck?"

"Yes?"

"Have you ever been in love?"

I'm not sure I have an answer. I had a serious girlfriend in high school—Cadence Pacetti—but I never said 'I love you' to her. We had a lot of sex, and we were the sweethearts of our high school class. I was going to get that D-1 scholarship, and we were going to—

But I didn't get the scholarship.

And then I joined the Navy.

I left Cadence behind in tears, and I moved on from her. From everyone.

And I fucked a lot of women—here and abroad. I mean, seriously... A *lot* of fucking women. Light-skinned, dark-skinned, slim, curvy, and everything in between.

Some I liked more than others.

Some I never saw again.

But only one did I love.

Her name was Amira. She was an Iraqi refugee, and I was just about to look into bringing her home with me when my tour was over—

When she was blown up by a suicide bomber.

I hadn't even told her I loved her.

And I did. Or I thought I did.

I couldn't mourn her. I didn't have time. A week after Amira died, I found myself in that foxhole with Ghost.

You can't have emotions in war. And yeah, we weren't technically at war, but it was a freaking war zone.

After Amira and after Ghost?

I turned my freaking emotions off.

It wasn't worth it.

"Are you going to answer me?" Aspen asks.

"I'm not sure how to."

"It's an easy question, Buck."

I shake my head, let out a soft scoff. "It's far from an easy question, baby."

"Yeah, I get it. It's not easy for me either."

"Are you saying you never loved Brandon?"

"I loved him. At that time, I would have sworn up-and-down that I loved him. Looking back though? I don't know."

"I understand."

"Do you?"

"Yes. There was a woman. In Iraq. Her name was...Amira."

"And you loved her?"

"I did, I think. But I never told her."

"Why not?"

"I don't know."

Except I do know. I didn't tell her because I was afraid. I was afraid of the feelings, and I was afraid of losing her. But I lost her anyway, and I wish she had gone to her grave knowing I loved her.

"Can you tell me about her?"

"No."

I expect her to balk, but she doesn't. She simply nods.

"I understand."

And in that moment, I know.

I know I've found the woman who gets me.

We've suffered through completely different scenarios, but she gets me. She understands me in a way I don't even understand myself.

One day I'll tell her about Amira.

One day I'll tell her about everything.

20

ASPEN

Amira is a beautiful name. And of course she was beautiful. Anyone who caught Buck's eye would be beautiful. She probably had dark hair, skin, and eyes, although perhaps not. I want to ask, but I don't.

He's not ready to talk about her.

And boy, do I understand.

Is Amira why he left the Navy? Or was it losing four teammates?

Or both? Or a combination of both and a lot of other things?

Whatever it ultimately was, it took its toll on this man—this strong and beautiful man.

"Buck?"

"Yeah?"

"I can't see my parents today. Maybe tomorrow."

"That's fine. Whatever you want."

"Can I tell you what I really want?"

"Of course."

"Would you lie here with me, let me lie in your arms?"

"Whatever you want." He pulls me into an embrace and then gently pushes me so we're both lying down. I snuggle into him, breathe in his spicy scent.

He groans, and I feel it more than hear it, as it flows throughout my body, making me feel...comforted.

Nurtured.

And... Dare I think it?

Loved.

We lie there, and I drift in and out of sleep. A few times Buck lets out a soft snore.

We don't move until it's nearly six o'clock, when Buck finally gets up, goes to the bathroom, and then returns.

"You hungry, baby?"

Baby. Warmth flows through me. I don't know what we are to each other, but I like that he calls me *baby*. It's part of what makes me feel safe and secure with him. Loved with him.

He doesn't love me. I'm not naïve. You don't fall in love in three days. But I feel *something* with him—something I never felt with Brandon.

Then again, with Brandon, I was a totally different person.

"Aspen?"

"Yeah?"

"I'd like to take you out to dinner."

"You did that last night."

"I know. I'd like to do it again. I'd like to spend some time with you. We don't need to talk. We can just eat."

"I don't have a lot of clothes, and you only have what's on your back."

"True." He clears his throat. "All right. Dinner in, then. The best room service has to offer. Do you like wine?"

"I do. Red more than white."

"Red it is. Maybe a nice burgundy." He pulls the room service menu off the desk. "You don't eat seafood... They have roast chicken, New York strip, and vegetarian pasta, also chicken piccata and veal scallopini."

"Roast chicken sounds good," I say. "Sounds...comforting."

"Perfect. Burgundy will go great with chicken. It's a lighter red."

"I do know. It's made out of Pinot Noir grapes."

"Hey, you know a little bit about wine."

"Only a little. It's not like we drank any fine wine on the island. My mom and dad like wine. Especially French wine."

"I'd like to meet them," he says.

I raise my eyebrows. Did I hear him right?

"I mean...when it's appropriate," he continues. "I get that you're not ready to see them yet. And of course, you're not ready for me to meet them. In fact, I don't ever need to meet them, Aspen. It's not like—"

"It's okay, Buck. I know you were just being polite."

"Right," he says. "Polite."

Buck calls room service. He orders the roast chicken for himself, as well, and a bottle of burgundy from a château I don't recognize. The chicken comes with mashed potatoes and green beans, and Buck orders cheesecake for dessert.

I don't have much of a sweet tooth, but cheesecake sounds good.

In fact, most food sounds good since I've been with Buck.

Perhaps I need someone as broken as I am to understand me.

But is he still holding a torch for Amira? The way Brandon seems to be holding a torch for me?

"Aspen?"

"Yeah?"

"I don't want to make you talk about this if you don't want to, but do you have any idea how you got taken in the first place?"

"No. My memories are kind of fuzzy, but I believe I was taken from a hotel room when we were in New York. For a game."

"Which hotel?"

"I... I mean I'm sure I could find out. Records like that are kept."

"I just wonder how all these women got taken. From what I can gather, most of them were in New York when it happened."

"That makes sense. The Wolfes are in New York., and it was their father that orchestrated all of this."

"Yes."

"Why do you need to know?"

"I guess I don't. But I want to know."

"Why?"

"Because whoever did this to you—whoever is responsible for putting you on that island—I want to make them pay."

"You don't need to do that."

"No. I do need to do it. For Amira. I couldn't make that bastard pay. He was a suicide bomber, so he was already dead. And damn... I couldn't make the fucker pay." Buck curls his hands into fists, and his jaw goes rigid.

He's angry. Still so angry at the person who took Amira from him.

"The guys responsible for me are gone anyway. Derek Wolfe is dead. The priest is dead."

"It's not that simple. Someone put those women in Derek Wolfe's path. In Katelyn's case, it was a cousin?"

"How would you know?"

Buck clears his throat. "She and I have talked, and I've talked to her boyfriend as well."

"Luke?"

"Yes."

"So you think someone alerted them to me. Sold me out?"

"I think so."

"Why? Why me?"

"You're beautiful and athletic and wonderful. So why *not* you, I suppose. But you had a whole team of volleyball players staying in the hotel."

"Some of whom are way more beautiful than I am," I say.

"I doubt that. But that's not my point. Someone zeroed in on you, and I want to know who put you in that position."

"Does it matter?" I sigh. "What's done is done. We can't erase the past. All we can do is forget about it and move on." And I laugh. I laugh out loud at my own words. "Forget about it? They'll tell me I can't. That I have to move forward and deal with the memories if I want to heal fully. I just don't want to, Buck. I don't want to remember."

"I understand. I wish I didn't remember."

"What happened to you, Buck? I can't even imagine."

"You don't want to imagine, but if anyone can imagine, it might be you, Aspen."

"At least I didn't have to fear for my life."

"I suppose not." Another throat clear.

"But there were women who disappeared from the island. Women who went on hunts and never came back."

"So they were killed?"

"None of us know for sure. We just assumed. Diamond always said they weren't allowed to kill us, but—"

"Diamond?"

"Yeah, she took care of us. We called her our house mother. No one really knows who she is."

Buck clears his throat a third time. "I know. I know who she is."

"You do? Who is she?"

"Her real name is Irene Lucent. Technically Irene Wolfe. She was Derek Wolfe's first wife."

My eyes nearly pop out of my face. "His wife? She *married* that maniac?"

"She did."

"All that time? She was a part of it?" I shake my head, nearly gasping out a sob. "She claimed to care about us, Buck. She—"

"Baby, she *did* care about you. She had her reasons for what she did."

"No reasons that were good enough."

"No reasons that either you or I can understand," he says. "She did it to protect her child."

"She had a kid?"

"Yes. Her son with Derek Wolfe. In fact, I guess we all owe that son our gratitude."

"Why?"

"Because he's the one. He's the one who killed the motherfucking bastard."

"Derek Wolfe was killed by his own son?"

"He was. His only legitimate son, actually. Derek Wolf never divorced Irene—Diamond. So his marriage to Constance Larson was never legitimate."

I raise my eyebrows. "The Wolfe siblings are illegitimate?"

"Technically, yes. But it doesn't really matter. They were still heirs to his fortune."

"And the other kid? What did he get?"

"He was supposed to get the island, that whole enterprise."

"My God, he was *in* on it?"

"He was."

"I don't understand any of this, Buck. What does it all mean?"

"I'm not sure myself, but Jordan—that's the name of the kid—turned on the old man at the end. Fell in love with his girlfriend. The model Fonda Burke."

My head is hurting. Pounding like a hammer. It's all too much information.

And I shriek.

I shriek like my head is about to explode.

21

BUCK

It's torture. Sheer torture hearing Aspen scream like that.

And I know what torture is.

This is sheer emotional torture. Sure, it's not hurting me physically—and I've been hurt physically beyond my limitations.

Mentally, emotionally...

I can't take it.

I've had to stop women from screaming before. I've had to knock them senseless to stop it.

But I won't do that to Aspen. I will never lay a hand on her to quiet her. Our lives are not in danger here.

But damn...

The shrieking...

It takes me back.

~

"Aмira," the woman chokes out in broken English. "My name is Amira."

Her cheek is swollen from where I slapped her to get her to stop screaming.

"I'm sorry, Amira. But I had to quiet you down. If they hear us —" I look over my shoulder. "If they hear us, they'll kill us both."

She nods, bites her bottom lip.

"Do you understand me? Do you understand English?"

She nods again.

"Okay, good. I only know a little bit of Arabic. Enough to get by. Or is Kurdish your language?"

"Kurdish," she says in her soft accent. "But my English is good."

Her voice... Even after all that screaming... It's so soft and gentle, like an angel's.

"I'll never lay a hand on you again, Amira. Trust me on that."

She nods.

I see trust in her big brown eyes. Why? She has no reason to trust me. I'm an American. A SEAL.

I look deeper—deeper into those eyes that have seen things no young woman should have to see.

And I understand.

She trusts me because if she doesn't, her life is over. Trusting me may be a mistake, but if it's not? I'm her best chance. If I don't kill her, someone else will.

"We need to be quiet," I tell her. "Later, you can tell me what happened to you, and I'll try to help. Right now we need to be quiet."

She nods. "I understand."

"Good."

She huddles into me, and I know why. She's seeking shelter. Comfort.

And I'm all that there is. She's chosen to place her trust in me *without knowing anything about me. She knows only that I'm the man who slapped her to get her to be quiet.*

I'm all she has.

And I vow, then and there, that she won't regret placing her trust in me.

~

IN THE END, I couldn't protect Amira. Her trust in me was misplaced.

I cannot fail Aspen the way I failed Amira. I just can't.

I could strike Aspen. I could strike her to make her stop screaming. But I won't. I'll never harm a hair on her head. We're not in danger here. The only danger is someone hearing her and calling the cops.

But she's shrieking. Crying and shrieking, and it's ripping my guts out.

So I do the only thing I can. I grab Aspen, pull her into me, crush her in a bear hug.

And I hope that the blanketing of my body will soothe her body and her mind.

22

ASPEN

Gloria Delgado is my roommate. She's my backup on the team, and she's good. Really good. To be honest? She's as good or better than I am. I was chosen simply for my size—size is still a factor for middle blocker, even though experts say it shouldn't be. I'm two inches taller than Gloria. Otherwise, we're equal as far as learned skill, experience, and natural ability.

We get along well. I like Gloria, and if she's jealous of my position, she's never made it clear.

She's in a relationship with another one of our teammates—Taylor Wallace. She and Taylor are out to dinner, and while the other girls invited me to an impromptu team dinner, I chose to stay in tonight.

I'm not feeling well. It started when I got off the plane at LaGuardia. I've been nauseated since, and although I know I need to eat, I figured room service would be a better option tonight, just in case I have to puke. If I'm nursing some kind of virus, I need to take care of myself—relax, get my immune system in gear—because I'm not going to miss the game tomorrow.

My phone buzzes.

It's a text from Gloria.

Just checking in. Are you feeling any better?

I quickly text her back. Still feel pretty funky. I'm going to order some dinner in.

Okay. Let me know if you need anything.

I text her back thanks *and a heart emoji.*

I grab the room service menu, but before I can take a look, I'm in the bathroom puking my guts into the toilet.

Geez. What could I have eaten? All I had on the plane was some Coke, and of course the obligatory bag of pretzels. Damn. Must be a virus, in which case I need to get it all out of me before tomorrow's game.

Once the heaves finally stop, I order a simple turkey sandwich from room service. White bread and turkey. That's about all my stomach can handle.

I lie on my bed, and twenty minutes later, someone knocks on my door.

Ugh. It takes all my strength just to get off the bed to get my sandwich from room service.

I open the door and—

A moment later, I'm waking up in a concrete room.

On the table next to me is a plate covered in a silver dome.

I jerk upward. Right. I'm in the hotel...

Except I'm not *in the hotel. My hotel room was not a concrete room with no windows.*

But I remove the dome from the plate on my table.

A turkey sandwich. A plain turkey sandwich on white. No condiments.

It's exactly what I ordered.

THE SCREAMING STOPS.

I'm enveloped in strength—as if a weighted blanket surrounds me.

Buck. Buck is holding me.

And I remember.

Damn it all to hell. I remember.

That screaming? It was coming from me. It was fueling this memory, and now that I have it?

I understand.

And I want to know more.

"Buck," I murmur.

He doesn't respond. He's murmuring in my ear. "It's okay, baby. It's all going to be okay."

"Buck." This time louder.

His hold on me lessens but only slightly. "Aspen?"

"I'm okay now. I'm sorry."

He loosens his grasp and pulls back slightly so that he meets my gaze. "You don't ever have to apologize to me. You understand that? Never."

"But the screaming..."

"Screaming is something you have to do. Sometimes it's just going to happen. I get it."

"I know you do. I'm sorry that you get it."

"Hey, what did I just say? No more apologies. Not to me."

"Okay."

"I want you to relax," he says. "Dinner will be here in a few more minutes. But you don't have to eat if you don't want to."

My stomach is hungry though. Surprisingly hungry.

"Buck, I remember something."

"Do you want to tell me about it?"

"Yeah. I think I do." I quickly relay the memory to him, all while swallowing back acid that wants to creep up my throat. But I'm determined. So freaking determined.

"So you were sick? But no one else on your team was?"

"Right. Not that I can recall, anyway. My roommate, Gloria, went out with her girlfriend. Some of the others on the team went out to dinner, and they invited me. But I chose to stay in because I wanted to be ready for the game the next day. I wanted whatever was making me sick to go away, and I figured the best way to make that happen was to stay in and rest."

"Yes, it would be. In fact..."

"What?"

Buck's forehead is wrinkled, and he threads his fingers through his long and unruly hair. "I don't want to alarm you, Aspen, but has it ever occurred to you that perhaps one of your teammates sold you out?"

My body goes cold. "No! They would never."

"Tell me about your roommate."

"We both played middle blocker. Gloria was my backup."

His eyebrows rise. "Your backup?"

"Yeah. I was the first team. She was my backup."

"How good was she?"

"She was as good as I was, and I'm pretty sure I got the position because I was a few inches taller."

Buck nods. "That makes sense on a volleyball team. How well did you know Gloria?"

"Pretty well. She was a nice girl. Honestly, I don't think she could've had anything to do with this."

"Sometimes people aren't who they appear to be," he says.

"Gloria? No. She was a devout Catholic. She did rosaries before bedtime. She was..."

"In a relationship with a woman?"

"Yeah, she was. But everyone was fine with it."

"Including Gloria? A devout Catholic?"

"Yeah. She was. She and I talked about it a few times. She had always been attracted to women, and she had talked to her priest about it on many occasions. Her church was fine with it. Her parents were fine with it. Everyone was fine with that."

"Okay. So Gloria didn't sell you out."

"I just can't believe that of her. The woman prayed for everyone. She prayed for the homeless, for lost puppies and kittens... I'm telling you she was devout."

"With you gone, Gloria would have your spot on the team."

"That's true. But she still wouldn't have done that to me. Gloria was... I don't know. She was seriously like the Miss Congeniality of our team. Everyone loved her, and she loved everyone."

"All right. Let's take Gloria out as a suspect for now then. You say you started feeling sick when you got off the plane?"

"Right."

"Who were you sitting with on the plane?"

"God. How am I supposed to remember that? This is all new, Buck."

"It's new to you now, but it's not new. You've opened up a database in your brain, Aspen. It's all there. You just have to access it. Were you sitting with Gloria?"

I think back, squeezing my eyes closed, trying to force an image into my mind. Who was I sitting with? The row comes into view. I'm on the aisle, and...Taylor. Taylor's across from me on the other aisle. She and Gloria always sat together on the plane.

"No, I was not sitting with Gloria. I was in an aisle seat because of my long legs. I can't remember who were in the other two seats."

"But you know for sure it wasn't Gloria."

"Yeah, I totally know for sure, because she was in the middle seat on the other side of the aisle. And her girlfriend, Taylor, was in the aisle seat across from me."

"Okay."

I rack my brain. Who was I sitting with? For the life of me, I can't make the faces appear in my mind. "Why does this matter, Buck?"

"Because you say you got sick after you got off the plane. Were you sick once you landed? At the airport? Or not until you got to your room?"

The wave of nausea... Yes. It was there. "Yeah. We got to baggage claim, and I was starting to feel nauseated."

"So that makes me think... If it was food poisoning, then it was something you ate on the plane. But all you had was a glass of Coke and a bag of pretzels. Pretzels aren't going to cause food poisoning. So it has to be the Coke, but that's unlikely as well, unless..."

"Unless what?"

"Unless somebody laced your Coke. Like with syrup of ipecac or something."

"Ipecac? That stuff they give little kids who've swallowed something bad?"

"Yep. That stuff."

"So you're thinking..."

"Right. Whoever was sitting next to you is the most likely culprit. If that's what happened."

"This is all a bunch of conjecture," I say.

"It is. But tell me this. By the time you woke up in the concrete room, were you still feeling sick?"

I drop my jaw. The turkey sandwich. I gobbled it up. "No. I wasn't. But I suppose it could've been days later."

"Could've been. But most likely it wasn't. Somebody made you sick so you wouldn't go out to dinner. And then somebody knew you ordered a turkey sandwich because you ended up getting a turkey sandwich in the concrete room."

"Yeah. I always thought that was kind of weird, but I didn't dwell on it. I mean, not with everything else that happened after."

"Totally understandable." He trails his finger over my cheek. "Damn."

"It's okay," I gulp.

He draws in a breath. "So we've got the hotel staff. Someone possibly monitoring your phone call or intercepting your room service order in another way. Someone knew you'd be expecting room service, so they knew you'd answer the door, and they could drug you."

"But I don't remember. I remember opening the door but then it's a blank."

"You don't remember if it was actually a hotel employee who brought your room service?"

"No, Buck. I wish I did, but I don't."

He sighs. "Okay. Who would want you off the team?"

"I don't know. We all got along."

"Once you were gone, Gloria got your position."

"I assume she did."

"She did." He holds up his phone.

I scan the screen. Wow. Buck has been searching this whole time we've been talking. Gloria Delgado took my position, and the team went on to win a championship that year. And the next.

Of course, who's to say they wouldn't have won with me as middle blocker?

"Still think it wasn't Gloria?" Buck says.

I don't reply.

I simply close my eyes, willing more memories to come back to me.

Because now... Now I want to remember.

I want to find out who did this to me.

And I want to make them pay.

23

BUCK

For the first time since I found Aspen at the train station, she has a different look on her face.

Her eyes are narrow, and her jaw set. Her hands are gripping each other with white knuckles. It's a look of determination—of anger and determination.

Something has awoken in her. I see it clearly because I've seen it so many times on my own face.

She wants revenge.

She wants her memories, and she wants revenge.

And I want revenge on her behalf.

God, I know better. Revenge is never the way. But sometimes...

Sometimes it's necessary.

"Aspen, baby."

"Yes?"

"We'll find them. We'll find them together."

She relaxes—slightly—and the whiteness of her knuckles softens. Her beautiful face, though? It's still a billboard for determination, for vengeance.

"Promise?" she says.

"Anything you need. I promise, baby. Anything you fucking need."

She walks toward the bed and sits down. "You said you ordered the food? It'll be here soon?"

"I did."

"Funny," she says. "I feel different. It's like... I don't want to answer the door and get the food from room service."

"That makes sense. You just had a big memory resurface. Answering the door for what you thought was room service is what led to your capture."

"Which means... I have to be the one to answer the door for room service."

He nods. "I understand. But I'll be right behind you."

"Thank you. I appreciate that."

God she's beautiful. So determined and beautiful, and damn... Revenge looks hot on her.

If only she could remember who was sitting next to her on the plane.

I'm getting ahead of myself. I don't even know if it was ipecac in her Coke. Or something else in her Coke. Or a simple virus.

But I have a hunch, and my hunches haven't failed me often in the past.

Sure, she could've been chosen randomly. Aspen is a beautiful woman—and a woman who would definitely be "worthy prey" as Derek Wolfe apparently liked to say.

Then again, any of the other members on the team would've also been worthy prey. I scroll through the team roster from before Aspen was taken. Gloria Delgado, her backup, is also beautiful—olive skin, dark hair and eyes.

Many of the other women are beautiful as well.

So perhaps it *was* just random. Someone knew her volleyball team was there—all of whom would be worthy prey—and Aspen just happened to be at the hotel while the rest were at dinner.

Except...I've been around the block enough to know things are rarely random.

Aspen was most likely chosen on purpose.

And again, the most logical culprit is Gloria Delgado, who would take Aspen's place on the team.

But Gloria—the good Catholic girl, Miss Congeniality of the team...

Aspen is right. It simply doesn't make sense.

And then it's hits me.

Gloria's girlfriend, Taylor. She was sitting in the aisle seat across from Aspen. If Aspen got up, went to the bathroom, and her Coke was still on her tray...

No. She would've moved her Coke to the next tray table while she got up so she could put her tray up.

Not Taylor, after all. If it was anyone, it had to be the person sitting in the middle seat next to Aspen.

Damn. Who was that person?

I can't force her to remember. Hell, mere hours ago she didn't want to remember anything.

But that's what happens when one memory surfaces. You have questions, and you need to know more. The curiosity of human beings overrides almost every other emotion.

Aspen wasn't curious before because she had no memories. But now? Now she has memories, and now she has questions.

And now she wants revenge.

"Aspen?"

"Yeah?"

"My hunch is that a team member did this to you."

"I know, but I just can't imagine any of my teammates would do such a thing. And even if they did have it out for me, how would they have known to get in touch with the degenerates who took me?"

She raises a good question, and I don't have an answer.

"We'll need to find out," I say, "if any of your teammates came into money after you were taken. Now, if whoever took you was smart, she hid her money well. But I can find out."

"How much did Derek Wolfe pay for the women?" she asks.

"Mere pennies to him," I say. "But to someone who needed money? Enough to make a difference. Usually around twenty-five or thirty thousand dollars."

"But we made decent money, Buck."

"That doesn't always matter," I tell her. "Someone may have needed an infusion of cash for an unforeseen reason."

She shakes her head. "My God. These people were absolutely evil."

"They were. And trust me, evil takes many forms. I've seen the worst of it."

Her gaze softens. "I'm so sorry. For everything you've been through."

I sit down next to her. "Please. Please stop saying you're sorry. It is what it is. What you went through, what I went through. Neither of us needs to apologize to anyone."

She lays her head on my shoulder. "You're right. Old habit I guess."

"Baby, that's a habit you need to break. You don't owe me or anyone an apology. You're not responsible for what happened to you, and you are certainly not responsible for what happened to me. There are a whole hell of a lot of people out there who owe us both an apology. Not that we'll ever get it."

"The Wolfes have apologized to me."

"I'm sure they have. They feel terrible about all of this. They feel responsible, like they should have known what was going on."

"Maybe they should have."

"You're right. Maybe they should have. But their old man kept it hidden very well. It wasn't a part of Wolfe Enterprises. Not at all."

"I don't blame them," she says. "Or I haven't. But now…"

"Now you need to blame someone because you're starting to remember. But the Wolfe siblings didn't do this to you."

"Then I want to find out who did."

"We can try. It will take time."

"I want to know now, Buck. I want to know who's responsible for this, and I want to make them pay."

"The people who are truly responsible for what happened you—Derek Wolfe and Father Jim Wilkins—are both dead."

"What about the men who hunted me? Who gave me the scars? Who took so much from me?"

"I can get names for you, Aspen, but none of that will matter."

"You're right. They don't matter. Most of them are probably locked up by now anyway. And if they're not, I don't ever want to see them again. That's not who I'm after."

"You want to know which of your teammates betrayed you."

"Yes, I do."

"And then what?"

"They will pay. They will simply pay."

Her voice is icy. Cold and icy.

It slithers up my spine, making my skin freeze.

I know then.

I know that I'm all in. As if I'm on a new SEAL assignment, to ferret out something and neutralize it.

That's how I'll attack this.

I'll find out who did this to Aspen.

Then I will neutralize them.

24

ASPEN

How do I get my memories back? I need to get back to Manhattan, back to Macy. She'll be thrilled that I finally want to get to the bottom of this.

Except she wants me to do it so I can heal, not get revenge on the person who wronged me.

I know in my heart that it wasn't Gloria.

I could be wrong, and if it turns out that I am, no one will be more surprised than I will be. But in the marrow of my bones, I know it wasn't her.

Taylor? Maybe.

Any of the others? Maybe.

But not Gloria.

I need to find Gloria, though. Maybe she'll remember who was sitting next to me on the plane. Are she and Taylor still together? Are they still playing for the team?

So much I don't know.

So much I didn't even want to know until now.

I jerk as a knock on the door interrupts my thoughts. I stand quickly, go to the door.

My skin chills as I reached for the doorknob, twist it, draw in a deep breath, and then open it.

I jump backwards in sheer instinct.

The suited hotel employee widens his eyes. "Room service?" he says hesitantly.

I draw in another deep breath. "Yes. Thank you."

I step out of the way, and he wheels the cart in.

"Over by the table, please," Buck says.

"Yes, sir."

The young man sets up the food for us and then hands the check to Buck. He scribbles his signature, and the young man thanks him and quickly leaves.

"You okay?" Buck asks.

"Yeah. I'm good." My heart is beating like a humming-bird's, but I'm breathing.

"You sure? You jumped back pretty far when you opened the door."

"Yeah, but I opened the door."

Buck smiles at me, and the chills I was feeling vanish and give way to the warmth of his comfort.

"You did. You opened the door, and now we're going to share a meal."

I'm oddly hungry. My appetite seems to have come back with the memories.

"Do you think I'm wrong?" I ask.

"About what?"

"About wanting to find who did this to me. To make them pay."

"Do you want to know what I think? Or what I'm supposed to think?"

"Both, I guess. Just one memory, Buck, and my entire atti-tude about this has changed. Before, I didn't want to remember. I thought it was best that I just move forward. But now? This one tiny memory has sparked a need in me. I need to know more."

"Is it a need for revenge?"

Be honest, I tell myself. *You have to be honest.* "Yes. So are you going to answer my question?"

"You already know the answer, baby." He shoves his hands in the pockets of his jeans. "What I'm supposed to think is that revenge is never worth it. The best revenge is to get past what they did to you and move on with your life. Be a success in spite of them. Now that attitude makes a lot of sense. Especially if you're passed over for a promotion at work because of a coworker's meddling. Or if a stupid driver cuts you off and then leaves the scene of the crime, while you drive into a ditch and do damage to your car. How much effort would you put into finding the person who did either of those? How much effort would you put into revenge?"

"You and I both know that what happened to me is nothing like—"

"Of course I know. There are certainly degrees here. What I'm supposed to feel is that revenge isn't necessary in any of these circumstances."

"And..."

"And in theory, I agree. Will it change what happened to you? Absolutely not. What happened happened, and you have to live with that."

"I know."

"What it can change is how *they* live. Now is that necessary in the grand scheme of things? No. Because it won't change what you went through."

"Is it wrong, then? That I want the person to pay? That I want them to hurt as I did?"

Buck pauses. He's thinking, and more than anything I want to know what's going through his head at this moment. It's good that he's thinking. He wants to give me a reasonable answer—a reasonable answer that will help me, not hinder me.

Finally—

"It's not wrong, baby. It's normal. It's human to want your abuser to suffer as you did."

"To be fair," I say, "this person never actually abused me. That honor belongs to Derek and the others."

"True. But whoever sold you out is responsible for *everything* that happened to you. Because if he or she had not done that, you wouldn't have gone through any of it."

I nod. I already know this. He doesn't have to spell it out for me.

"Still," I say, "I should be the bigger person, right? I should move forward, not backward. Because as you say, none of it changes what I've been through."

"None of it changes what you've been through," he echoes. "But...perhaps it will give you some peace to know the person who began all of this will now pay the price. Plus, whoever it is will never be able to harm anyone else."

Hmm. Interesting. No one else would be harmed. The island is now history and Derek Wolfe and Father Jim Wilkins are dead and buried, but whoever began the process for me obviously has no problem putting others in harm's way.

Buck makes it sound almost...noble.

I certainly don't want anyone else to be harmed in any way.

Except if I'm honest with myself, my primary reason for finding this person isn't to assure the safety of others.

Buck is right.
I want this person to pay.
And if I find out Gloria *was* behind all of this?
Then damn her. Damn the good Catholic girl.
She will fucking pay.

25

BUCK

I recognize the look in Aspen's eyes.

I've seen it on the battlefield.

I've seen it in my friends, teammates, fellow SEALs.

And I've seen it in the fucking mirror.

In my own damned eyes.

Vengeance.

Such a simple word... But it can turn a person's life upside down.

I went looking for vengeance not long ago—looking for the man who had wronged my sister. But when I found him? He wasn't the same man.

That didn't matter to me, of course. But what did matter to me was the woman—his woman. She had saved him.

And she also saved me.

Katelyn. Katelyn Brooks is her name.

The man I was looking for? Lucifer Charles Ashton the third. Street name Lucifer Raven. He was the right-hand man to one of the most notorious drug lords in LA, and he was also the man who harmed my sister. He was mentally and emotionally abusive, sometimes physically abusive as well, and when he disappeared...I knew... I knew in the deepest recesses of my soul that he was still alive, and I set out to find him.

And when I *did* find him?

I also found his new woman. His Katelyn. Katelyn who swore up and down that he was amazing and would never harm another living soul.

Can people change?

I never believed it.

But I believe it now. Lucifer—now known as Luke Johnson—proved it. He got away from the drug business, turned canary and sold out some of his cohorts. I normally hate narcs, but these people had to go down. Luke did it with the help of his old man, who has old money and lots of connections. But what truly changed him? He got off alcohol. Lucifer Raven was an alcoholic. And then he met Katelyn.

A big part of me still wants to see the man dead and buried. A big part of me still wants to pummel him, take out all my aggressions on him the way he took his out on my sister.

But I don't. I don't because of Katelyn. Katelyn, who was also held on Derek Wolfe's island and who is a very special woman, and she sees something in Luke Johnson—something I'll never see. Something I don't want to see.

But I witnessed it. I witnessed how he was willing to give his life for hers.

So I gave him back his life. It still sticks in my craw. I can't deny it. But somehow, he makes Katelyn Brooks happy. I've never bought into the old adage that a good woman can change any man. I think that's bullshit.

But whatever happened to Lucifer Raven, he's now in my debt.

He said as much because of how I protected Katelyn when all three of us were in pretty damned hot water.

I didn't ever plan on cashing in on that debt.

But for Aspen?

I'll cash in.

Vengeance...

What a fucking beautiful and ugly word.

"You going to join me?" Aspen asks from the couch, where she's slicing the roast chicken.

I sit down next to her. "Yeah. I am."

We eat in silence. Silence that's so thick, I'm convinced I can slice my steak knife through it and see it part like the freaking Red Sea.

But Aspen is eating. She's devouring, actually. This memory has sparked something in her—and I'm not sure if it's good or bad, to be honest.

When I finish the last morsel on my plate, I wipe my lips with my napkin and turn to her. "Do you want to see your parents tomorrow?"

She shakes her head instantly—almost too quickly. "No."

"But isn't that the reason you came out here? To see Brandon and then your parents?"

"And the mountains. But things change, Buck."

Her eyes again. Those beautiful brown eyes with long ebony lashes... But in them I see only vengeance.

The need for revenge.

And I feel it as well. Damn! I don't want to feel it, but I do. It exudes off Aspen and into me, and I need revenge against her perpetrators as much as she does.

Every time I feel this way...

God, no.

Every time in the past that I felt this way?

Someone died.

Someone I cared about died.

Except for the last time. When I went after Lucifer Raven. No one died on my watch. Emily is safe on Billionaire Island. Katelyn is safe. Even Kingsford Winston, the drug lord we took down that day, is safe in a fucking prison cell.

No one died that day.

So perhaps no one will die this time.

I don't want any more deaths on my conscience.

"Aspen, baby, you need to see your parents."

"Who says? You? Macy? My parents? You know what? The only opinion that matters is my own."

"Your parents need to see you. They need to see you alive."

"They know I'm alive. I've spoken to them."

"It's not the same thing, and you know it. They love you."

"I love them too. But they don't want to see me like this."

"Look," I say. "I'm not a father myself, so I can't speak for how they're feeling. But from what I understand about parents and their children, they won't care that you've changed. The fact that you're alive... It's like a miracle to them, and they need to see it. They need to see you with their own eyes."

She sighs then. "I'm an only child. Their one and only."

"An even better reason."

"All right. I'll see them tomorrow. Because..."

"Because why?"

"Because, Buck, it may be the last time I can see them alive."

An invisible sword slices through me. "What the hell are you talking about?"

Her face goes rigid, her countenance stoic. "Whoever did this to me is going down, Buck. I'll do it with or without your help, but they're going down, and if I have to go down with them, so be it."

26

ASPEN

The words leave my mouth before I can think them through, but even as I hear myself say them, I know their truth.

Inside my heart—my soul—I know their truth.

For the first time I'm feeling alive. So damned alive.

I feel like I have a purpose now. To find whoever did this to me and take them down no matter what the cost.

But Buck is right about one thing. I do need to see my parents. I need to let them believe that I'm okay.

Whether I am or not.

I turn to him, cup both his cheeks, and let his stubble scrape my palms.

Then I bring his mouth to mine.

I don't have to prod him or pressure him. He responds to my kiss immediately, and what a kiss it is. Open-mouthed and heavenly. Tongues, teeth, lips...

It's a raucous, ravaging kiss.

Again, I feel so alive. So alive and perfect and wonderful.

I need him. I want him. I want him to see who I am.

My whole body, with all its scars and missing parts.

And God... I want to see *his* body. His majestic and perfect body.

Except—

He breaks the kiss.

My fingers go instantly to my lips. They're stinging. They're stinging in a wonderful way, and I whimper at the loss of his lips on mine.

"Baby..." he growls.

"Please, Buck. I want you. I need you. Please..."

"I shouldn't have ever—"

"Don't say that." I touch his lips.

He kisses my fingertips and then brushes my hand away. "You have no idea how much I want you."

"I think I do."

"Aspen, you're hell-bent on revenge right now. It's not sex you want."

"No, it's you. I want *you*, Buck. You. I want your mouth back on mine. I want it now."

He groans, but then he crushes our lips together.

Crazy. As much as my body was used and abused and tortured—how is it that I want sex now?

It's not the sex.

It's the man. *This* man. His six three to my six feet, and this couch—it's too small for us. Yet I don't want to break the kiss to lead him to the bed.

No. It's imperative that our mouths stay together. I don't know why, but it is. His kisses are rough, passionate, raw, and feral. And they... God, they drive me wild.

There was no kissing on the island. None. It wasn't forbidden, but those degenerates weren't after kissing. They came to hunt. To abuse, to torture.

Not to kiss. Kissing was way too intimate.

And God, I've missed kissing.

Even so... No one has ever kissed me like Buck Moreno. Not Brandon or anyone else.

And this kiss? This kiss is more than a simple meeting of mouths. It's a moment of truth. It's showing me that I can be a real person again.

That I can have my life back.

And that I can have what I long for.

Revenge.

I want to take out all my frustrations on Buck's body, but I don't want to use him. He has to want this too, and judging by his kiss? He does.

I won't be the one to break the kiss, but—

He breaks it, my mouth stinging and tingling again.

"Bed," he says gruffly. Then he picks me up, throws me over his shoulder as if I were nothing more than a sack of potatoes, and takes me to the bed.

He lays me down on my back, pulls off my shoes and jeans. He takes off his shirt, and then he hovers above me, kisses my mouth, and then slowly pulls up my shirt.

He's seen me naked, but now he's going to look. Truly *look* at me.

He's going to see what they did to me.

All the scars... The missing nipple...

I want to bring myself to care. To tell him not to look. But I can't.

Because I want him more than I want to ease the ache of embarrassment.

Up my shirt goes, sliding slowly, until he pulls it over my head. Now only my bra separates me from him seeing everything, looking at everything.

He touches me then, trails his fingers over all the scars on my belly, leaving sparks in his wake. My bra still hides the most wretched part. He leans down, slides his lips where his fingers were, caressing each scar, kissing it, licking it, making my capillaries burst with heat and energy.

"So beautiful," he murmurs.

Beautiful? My scars?

I'm still me. But I'm no longer beautiful. I'm not sure I ever was.

"God, you are." As if he's responding.

I know I didn't speak aloud. He's reading my mind, which is a little frightening but also comforting.

He moves upward, kisses and caresses the tops of my breasts, and then he reaches under me and unsnaps my bra.

I suck in a breath.

Will he be disgusted?

He pulls my bra off, and—

"Oh, baby..."

I turn my head, unable to meet his gaze.

But he cups my cheek, brings my gaze back to his.

"You're beautiful," he says.

"Buck..."

"Listen to me. You are a beautiful woman, Aspen, and I want you right now more than I've ever wanted anyone. Believe that."

He moves downward then, to my right areola that is nippleless, and he kisses it. He licks it. He caresses it.

My phantom nipple emerges, stretching outward, wanting him. Needing him.

He moves to my other nipple then, sucks it between his lips, tugs on it gently.

A soft sigh escapes my throat.

I relish the attention to my breasts, but too soon he lets the nipple drop, returns to my lips, and kisses me deeply.

We kiss for a few timeless moments, and then he breaks it, licking first my upper and then my lower lip.

"So beautiful. Never forget that." His mouth meets mine again.

We kiss, we kiss, we kiss... He ravages my mouth, and then, without any forewarning, he breaks the kiss and flips me over in one swift move. He brings me to my hands and knees, and I'm still wearing my panties.

"Beautiful ass," he growls. He pulls my panties over my hips, my thighs, and then off me. Before I know it, his tongue is between my cheeks, and he's eating me. Licking from my clit all the way up to my ass.

My God, my God. Feels so, so good. I shudder, tremble beneath his tongue and lips.

"So sweet," he growls. "God, you taste good."

In another instant, I'm again on my back, my legs spread, and he's noshing at me. Pushing my thighs forward so that I'm open to him. Completely open. He sucks me hard and fast, making succulent noises as he tugs on my clit. He slides a finger inside me, and then another. He strokes me gently as he continues sucking on my clit, and—

A climax rips through me, and I bring my hands to my breasts, tugging on my left nipple and caressing the areola on my right.

"That's it, baby. Come for me. Come all over my face."

The passion, the amazing emotion. How long has it been? How long has it been since I've had a climax like this?

And something dawns on me. I've *never* had a climax like this. Not with Brandon or anyone else.

This is a first for me. An explosive first, and I sure as hell don't want it to be the last.

Buck is still wearing his jeans, but I want to see him. I want to see all of him. So I gaze at him, at his broad, tanned shoulders, at his chest when he lifts his chin, glistening with my juices.

"Let me see you," I say.

"Not yet." He returns to my pussy.

Before I know it, I'm exploding again, and then again.

I've never had a multiple orgasm before. Never in my life.

But never in my life have I had Buck Moreno.

"Buck, please... No more... I can't take anymore..."

"Oh, you can. And you *will*."

27

BUCK

She tastes like sugar and spice. The sweetness of sugarcane with some cayenne pepper thrown in. Sugar and spice, but not everything nice.

Sugar and spice with an edge.

She's fucking delicious.

"Please..." she begs.

But I'm going to get one more out of her. She's so hot, and even I can't believe how responsive she is. Especially after all she's been through.

But I can do it. I can pull another one out of her.

That's how determined I am.

I fuck her with my two fingers, massage her G spot, and yeah... That gets her going. Her thighs are touching her chest now, and she's holding them open, leaving her pussy on full display.

Her shiny asshole beckons, but that will have to wait. No way is she ready for anything there.

But she *is* ready for one more orgasm, and I will force it out of her.

Her clit is still swollen, still throbbing, and the walls of her vagina are still pulsing.

When they finally slow, I go in for the kill. I suck her hard clit between my lips, pulling, tugging, all the while massaging that G spot and fucking her with my fingers.

Fast, fast, fast. My fingers piston in and out of her pussy, and just when I know she's ready to jump, I tug harder.

"Oh my God!"

Yes, there it is. The fourth climax. And it's a big one.

"Yes, baby. Come again. Come for me." I drill in and out of her pussy hard, fast, faster, faster faster...

She continues shrieking, groaning, moaning. My name drips from her lips.

Buck! Buck! Buck!

And God, my name has never sounded sweeter.

So fucking beautiful.

Even with all the scars—the missing nipple.

God, what did they do to her?

Still... Her body is more beautiful than any I've ever seen. Even the most beautiful Playboy centerfield or the hottest supermodel...

Aspen makes them all look average.

Emotion roils through me—comes up from the depths of my belly and settles in my heart.

It scares me. It scares the hell out of me, but right now, I have to go with it. I have to—

"Aspen, I—"

I stop.

I stop myself. She's not ready to hear what I have to say.

Hell, *I'm* not ready to hear what I have to say.

Too soon. It doesn't make any sense.

Finally, she comes down from the fourth climax. I slow

my fingers, enjoy the sweet suction of her pussy around them, and then I withdraw.

I hover over her then and gaze at her beautiful face. Her eyes are closed, her lips glistening, and beads of sweat have emerged around her hairline.

I look again at her breasts, at the right one that is missing a nipple.

And I vow then and there.

I will help her find the psychopath who started this process. I will help her find who did this.

And I will make them pay.

Then I shove my cock inside her.

Sweet sanctuary.

Sweet home.

Home fucking sweet fucking home.

She's still pulsing lightly from the last orgasm, and it's heaven against my cock.

I'm not wearing a condom, but I'm not worried. She's clean and on the pill, and I know I'm clean. She doesn't seem to be worried either because she doesn't say anything.

So I fuck her. First slowly, but I know that won't last long.

Soon I want more. So I fuck her hard. I fuck her fast.

Then, she opens her eyes. "Buck."

"Yeah, baby?"

"Please. I want to get on top. I want to feel... I want to feel in control."

Works for me. I roll us over until she's on top of me, straddling me.

I stare at her. Regard her beautiful body, her two tits bouncing.

She fucks me hard at first, but then she slows down, and in some strange maneuver, her legs are now in front of my hips, and her arms are holding her up as she fucks me. Damn, she's flexible. Most women couldn't do this. But I get why she's doing it. It's putting pressure on her G spot.

She's bracing herself to come again.

My God, this woman is amazing.

She's going slowly, and I have a bird's eye view of her beautiful clit. A bird's eye view of my dick gliding in and out of her pussy.

And I swear to God, I just got harder.

"Fuck, baby," I grit out. "Holy fuck."

She closes her eyes again, continues what I swear must be patented moves. I've never experienced anything like this.

"How do you make your body do that?"

"I've always been"—she gasps—"flexible."

Flexible? She gives the word flexible new meaning.

In a flash, she's changed positions again. She's straddling me, her ass facing me now. I can't help myself. I wet my finger in my mouth, and then I touch her asshole.

She gasps for moment…and I freeze.

But then she continues riding me. She didn't tell me to stop.

So I don't stop.

I massage that tight little asshole with my finger, and it takes every bit of strength I possess not to breach that tight rim and finger her.

She fucks me hard, fucks me fast, and then, in another flash of movements, she's sitting on me sideways, moving up and down, with only her legs doing the work. Her arms are at her sides.

Damn, she's strong. And she probably only got stronger on that island.

The sensation is novel. And wonderful. I've never felt a

woman's pussy from this angle, and it's amazing. Different and erotic and amazing.

But before I can get much more of it, she's back, straddling me, gazing down in my eyes.

"Touch me," she says. "Please, Buck. Touch my clit."

I wet my finger again, smooth it over the hard knob—

And she explodes.

She explodes all over my cock as she fucks me, milking me, contracting around me.

I'm not sure how I've lasted this long, but now? I explode with her. I empty myself into her sweet pussy.

And I swear to God...

I will never fuck another woman.

Aspen. Aspen is my forever.

28

ASPEN

So much more I want to do to him.

So many more positions I want to try.

I've never been this into sex in my life. How can I be now? After everything I've been through? It makes no sense, but I've decided to go with it.

Buck is the most magnificent man I've ever seen. Now that we're both coming down from an orgasm, I rake my gaze over his body.

I take in all his scars.

And if it's possible... I think he's more scarred than I am.

He's not missing a nipple, of course, but he does have a stab mark that just missed his nipple by a few millimeters. He has more stab marks on his abdomen, plus a few bullet wounds.

And then on his back...

His tattoo. His memorial to his fallen friends—along with scars that could only have come from a leather whip.

I should know.

I have them too.

"You're beautiful," I say, sliding my fingers over a scar across his chest.

"God, so are you. So fucking beautiful."

I open my mouth, ready to ask him if I'm still beautiful without a nipple...but then I choose to stay silent. He said I'm beautiful. He's seen all of me, and he still says I'm beautiful.

He touches me, cups my breast, thumbs my one remaining nipple and the area where the other one would be. He doesn't ask any questions. Does he want me to volunteer the information?

He'll be waiting a long time then.

I don't remember most of what I endured on that island, but that time?

That time, I remember with vivid clarity.

DIAMOND GAVE *me Nike running shoes this time.*

"Why?" I ask her

"I just do what I'm told, Garnet. But use them. Use them to the best of your ability."

I nod. The running shoes mean only one thing. Whoever is hunting me today is as athletic as I am—probably more so.

After all, whoever it is hasn't been through hell for the last couple years.

In truth though? I'm probably in the best shape of my life. Running from these freaks, using my brain and hiding when I can, has kept me in better shape than the most vigorous volleyball training.

Running shoes.

"I'll need socks," I say.

"Yes, they're inside the shoes."

Sure enough, balled in the toe of each shoe is an athletic ankle sock.

"Do I get anything else? Clothes?"

She shakes her head. "I'm afraid not. Just the shoes."

Whoever is going to catch me wants me to run. He wants me to run hard. Once he captures me, he doesn't want to be bothered with having to take off my clothes.

Great. Just great.

A few of the girls have learned to have a sense of humor about all of this.

I have not.

I envy them sometimes. Their laughter. I'm not sure I'll ever laugh again.

"Anything else you can tell me?" I ask Diamond.

"I wish I could, Garnet. They only tell me very little."

"I can assume that whoever is going to hunt me wants a challenge," I say. "Otherwise no shoes."

She nods but says nothing.

"So my assumption is correct?"

"I've said all I can say."

"Fine. I understand."

"Garnet?" she says.

"Yes?"

"Run. Run hard and run fast. As fast as you fucking can."

I widen my eyes. Diamond doesn't normally use profanity, so she means what she says.

"I will," I reply.

I will anyway, but now?

I really will.

An anvil lodges in my gut. No. Not now. I can't have anything weighing me down.

I breathe in and out as slowly as I can, and though I succeed in dislodging the imaginary anvil, my heart flutters rapidly.

Adrenaline. A surge of adrenaline.

That's what I need, and my body never fails me.

Please, don't fail me now.

29

BUCK

The next morning we arrive at Aspen's parents' home in Denver proper. It's a red brick two story with a gorgeous green lawn, obviously well cared for. Aspen is quiet in the seat next to me, and her bottom lip is red from her constant biting.

She looks beautiful, though. Her face bears no scars from her time in captivity.

"You want me to go in with you?"

"No," she replies.

"Are you sure?" Things didn't go as planned with Brandon, and I want to be there for her this time if she needs me.

"I'm sure. She clicks the door handle of the passenger side of the rental car. Then she turns to me. "I changed my mind. I'd like you to come in. I don't think I can do this alone."

I touch her soft cheek. "You understand they're going to want you to talk. They're going to want to hug you and kiss you and tell them the whole story."

"That's why I need you there. I don't *know* the whole story, Buck. I have fragments of memories, sure. And even those I don't want to share with my parents. How can I tell them what happened to me?"

"They know, baby. They already know what happened to you, or they can at least wager a good guess. It probably makes them sick inside."

"I'm sure it does. I don't want them to feel that way, which is part of the reason why I've resisted seeing them. But I do have to see them, and it has to be today."

I don't reply. I don't want to think about the words Aspen said to me last night—that this may be the last time her parents see her alive.

This is a woman who saved herself. Who got through literal hell on earth and lived to tell about it. How can she be so indifferent about life?

Is it really more important to make the person who began this process pay than it is for her to live?

I know how she's feeling. God, I've been there. There were times I wanted to die. There were times I wanted to die the most horrific death possible as payment for the inability to save my friends.

So I get it. I get it more than Aspen knows. But I moved through it, and she must move through it as well.

Finding the person who ultimately tried to destroy her isn't worth her *life*.

But I can't think about that now. I have to be strong for Aspen. I have to accompany her into her parents' home, where they won't know me.

They don't want to see me. They want to see Aspen.

But if she needs me, I'll be there. Maybe she'll be comfortable enough that I can leave, wait in the car.

We both exit the car and walk up to the front door.

She turns to me. "What if they're not home?"

"It's Sunday. Where would they be?"

"At church?"

"Are your parents big churchgoers?"

She bites her lip again, and then she shakes her head. "On Easter. Christmas Eve. That's about it."

"Then they're probably here today." I raise my fist to knock on the door.

She grabs it.

"We'll take all the time you need," I say. "We can stand here for as long as you want."

But behind the door, a dog barks.

So it will only be a matter of time until someone—

The door opens.

The woman—only slightly shorter than Aspen and wearing jeans covered in an apron—gasps as the dog—a Golden Retriever—continues to bark.

"Hi, Mom." Aspen's voice shakes, but just a little.

"Hush, Ricky," the woman says to the dog. Then she pulls Aspen into an embrace. Tears squeeze from her closed eyes. "Oh my God, baby tree. Thank God you finally came home." Then she looks over her shoulder. "Darnell! Hurry! She's home! Our baby tree is home!"

Baby tree? Seems to me she said she wasn't named after the Aspen trees. Perhaps the nickname means something else.

The woman—most definitely Aspen's mother—doesn't let go.

A few seconds later, a muscled older man, graying at the temples and with slightly darker skin than both Aspen and her mother, walks out briskly from what appears to be a kitchen.

"Lisa? She's really— Oh my God!"

I lean against the wall next to the open door, trying to blend in with the surroundings. Of course I never blend in anywhere. I'm huge.

But I'm not as huge as Aspen's father. The man's clearly in his late fifties or early sixties, but he's got a few inches on me and shoulders even broader than mine. This is where Aspen got her athletic ability. From this man.

Aspen's father—Darnell, apparently—looks me up and down. "Who the hell are you?"

Yeah, so much for fading into the woodwork. Never works for me. I take a few steps forward and hold out my hand. "Buck Moreno. I'm Aspen's security."

His eyes widen slightly. "Who hired you?"

"The Wolfe family."

"The Wolfe family? Who kept my daughter against her will for—"

I get the feeling I shouldn't interrupt this bear of a man, but I do anyway. "That was their father, Derek Wolf. His children had nothing to do with that. In fact, they're doing everything they can to make sure all the women harmed by their father heal, including your daughter."

He scowls. "Sure. Tell them to expect a lawsuit soon."

"No need to file any lawsuit," I say. "They'll give you whatever you need. They'll give Aspen whatever she needs. They take this responsibility seriously."

"Oh?"

"Yes."

I've overstepped my bounds a little. I have no idea if the Wolfe family is willing to pay off the families of the victimized women. Still, I don't want this guy suing the Wolfes. They're good people.

Aspen finally disentangles herself from her mother. "No,

Daddy. I don't want you to sue the Wolfes. None of this was their fault."

"I would be doing it for you, little tree."

"They've given me everything I need. Endless therapy, a place to live, money until I can make a living on my own."

"You shouldn't have to work another day in your life after what you've been through," Darnell growls.

"For God's sake, Darnell," Lisa says. "Our daughter is home. Let's focus on that. She's home. She's alive. And she looks... Little tree, you look beautiful." She sniffles and then turns to me. "What did you say your name was? Buck?"

"Yes, ma'am."

"Thank you for bringing Aspen back to us. But if you don't mind..."

"No, Mama. I want him to stay."

"But little tree, we have so much to talk about. Your room is just as you left it. We didn't change a thing."

"Oh, Mama..."

"We just couldn't. We always wondered... We never lost hope... Everyone else told us to accept the fact that you were dead, but I knew better. A mother knows in her heart."

Darnell clears his throat. "I just started a new pot of coffee in the kitchen, if either of you would like some."

"Sure, Daddy," Aspen says. "That would be nice."

Lisa gestures to the living room to our left. "Have a seat. Please. Darnell will bring the coffee in."

I take a seat in a chair so that Aspen can sit with her mother on the sofa. The room is sparsely decorated, and I like it. Not a lot of knick knacks to collect dust. The furniture is boxy, as if it all came from Ikea, and it's in dark blues and grays.

Darnell returns with the tray holding a coffee pot and mugs. Such a big guy carrying coffee. It's almost comical.

He sets the tray down on the coffee table and proceeds to pour a mug of coffee for each of us.

"You still take your coffee black, little tree?"

Aspen nods.

"And you?" He gestures to me.

"Black as well. Thank you." I take a sip of coffee from the mug he hands me.

"Can I convince you to come to the basement with me?" Darnell asks. "I have some great firearms collections."

I lift my eyebrows.

"I'd like to give Lisa some time with our daughter. If you don't mind."

I know what this is about. Sure, I think he *does* want to give his wife time with her daughter. I also think he wants to find out more about me.

Okay. I'm game. If I were Aspen's father, I'd probably want the same thing. I rise. "Are you okay if I leave, Aspen?"

She nods. "I'm fine."

"All right then," I say to her father. "Let's see what you've got."

He has no way of knowing I'm a Navy SEAL and that I've seen pretty much every firearm in the world. I follow him through the kitchen and dining area down a staircase into a finished basement.

He wasn't kidding. The walls are lined with firearm after firearm, and some are antiques.

For a moment I wonder if he's brought me down here to kill me.

"You look like a man who knows guns," he says.

"I am. I'm interested in how you know that."

"I can tell. A certain look in a man's eye. Or even a woman's eye. You get to know it after a while."

He's not wrong. It's not something I ever noticed, but now, looking at him, I see the same. Of course, my other clue is the mass of guns lining his walls.

"Were you in the military?" I ask.

"Sure as hell was. Navy SEAL." He drops his gaze to the Budweiser on my forearm. "That's why I invited you down here. I see you were as well."

Damn. Darnell was a SEAL. Why didn't Aspen mention that? I'll ask her later.

"I was," I say.

"I bet you have some stories to tell."

"I'm sure you do as well."

"Iraq," he says. "Desert Storm and Desert Shield."

"Afghanistan."

The thing is, we may both have stories to tell, but neither of us is going to tell them. We don't talk about that shit.

"It gratifies me to know you're a brother," he says. "Thank you. For taking care of Aspen."

"My pleasure."

He raises his eyebrows at me. "A pleasure?"

Man, did that sound all "I'm having sex with your daughter?"

I don't think so. Aspen *is* a pleasure. She's lovely. Strong and willful and beautiful and smart.

"Yes, she's a very nice young woman."

"Listen, she's a beautiful girl. You just keep your hands to yourself."

I raise one eyebrow at him. "I'm her security guard."

"Make sure it stays that way." He clears his throat. "I don't want any more harm coming to my little girl."

His eyes have a hard look. An "I'm going to make them pay" look. Hell, I know the look. I've seen it in my own eyes.

This dude is bigger than I am and has a wall full of guns. God help the man who crosses his path.

"Mr. Davis—"

"Darnell," he says. "Or Captain, to a fellow SEAL. Or sir."

If we were in the trenches, it would be sir, as he outranks me.

But we're not in the trenches, and I don't want to think about rank.

I clear my throat. "Why do you call Aspen little tree and baby tree?"

His dark eyes soften—as much as they can in a room full of weaponry. "She was a skinny child, always the tallest, plus her name is Aspen, though it's a family name. Little tree seemed to fit. For Lisa, it's baby tree sometimes. Aspen never seemed to mind, so we've never stopped calling her that, though she's far from little anymore."

I smile without meaning to. The image of Aspen as a skinny little girl doesn't jibe with who she is now. Not at all. She's lean but not skinny, muscular but not bulky. She's perfect.

I wait for him to ask me about my nickname, but he doesn't. Maybe he thinks Buck is my given name. Or maybe he doesn't care. Probably the latter.

I gaze around the wood paneled walls again, taking in the amazing collection. "Darnell, have you done any investigation on your own?"

"I've been investigating this since she disappeared," he says. "But she disappeared into thin air. Whoever did it covered their tracks—or had them covered—very well. Do you have any new information?"

"Nothing new, but I'm pretty sure it was one of her team-mates who sold her out."

"I'm pretty convinced of the same," Darnell says.

"Have you found any evidence?"

"The only information I've got so far is the manifestation from the flight that took them into Manhattan."

"You have that? Just the manifestation, or do you have a seating chart from the flight itself?"

"I have a contact at the FAA. He got everything for me."

"That's great! The person who was sitting next to Aspen might have poisoned her drink."

Darnell's eyes spark with fire. "So that's how this all started?"

"We don't know for sure, and there's no way to prove it now." I briefly fill him in on my hypothesis.

"Damn. I never thought I'd want to harm a woman in my life, but if one of those volleyball bitches did this to my little girl..." His fingers curl into fists.

"We have to prove it first."

"So we prove it," he says.

"Exactly how? You want to question each of them?"

"For starters, just the ones who were sitting with her on the plane and the one who took her position on the team."

"It was so long ago. They'll lie."

"They won't lie," he says, "because I'll be holding an AR-15 to their heads when we talk. They'll spill their guts like a fucking geyser."

I meet Darnell's gaze. His eyes hold the same determined fire as his daughter's.

Good.

We understand each other.

We understand each other very well.

30

ASPEN

I want to talk to my mother. I do. But she keeps going from sobbing to weeping, to hugging me close to her, to sobbing again.

I do my best to understand amidst the guilt I feel for not coming sooner, and for not letting them visit me at the retreat center or in Manhattan.

"Mom," I say.

She sniffles, and her nose is nearly raw. "Yes?"

"Please. Please, let's talk. I know you have questions."

"No. No questions. I'm just glad you're here." She grabs onto me again.

"Okay. I get it. You just want to be with me. I can't stay very long."

"Why not? You're home now."

"They're expecting me back in Manhattan. I have a therapist there."

"We'll find you a therapist here. The best money can buy."

"I don't need money for therapy. Macy—she's my therapist in Manhattan—is paid for by the Wolfe family."

"Well, you no longer need Macy. We'll get you a therapist here."

"Mom, I don't have any health insurance right now, and I know you and Dad don't have extra money lying around to get me the kind of help I need."

"Money doesn't matter, Aspen. You're home now. I promise you'll get the help you need."

If I truly wanted to stay home, I know the Wolfe family would pay for my therapy here. They'd pay for whatever I need. But...I don't want to stay here. Especially now that I know Brandon still has feelings for me, and especially because...

I have other things I need to do.

I need to figure out who betrayed me.

My father and Buck return from the basement. Buck doesn't look any worse for the wear. I never thought I'd meet a man tougher than my dad, but Buck, though not quite as tall and broad, is as tough or tougher.

"Little tree," Dad says, "your friend here and I have decided to join forces."

Mom stands then. "What the hell are you talking about, Darnell? No one is joining forces with anyone."

"Lisa, we may be able to put this to rest once and for all."

"It's *been* put to rest. Aspen is home. She's alive, and she's safe. Let's leave it at that."

Unfortunately, I have to intervene. I stand, meet my mother's gaze. "No, Mom. I need to know. I need to know who set this whole thing in motion. I'm almost positive it was one of my teammates."

"Oh, little tree... Please... You're safe now. Safe at home where you belong. Please, don't put yourself in harm's way."

"I won't be in harm's way, Mom. I just need to find out. I need to investigate. Talk to all of my teammates."

"How on earth will you ever track them down?"

"A lot of them probably still play for the team."

"About half of them are still on the team," Dad says.

"Christ, Darnell. You've been looking into this?"

"Yes, Lisa, I have. This is our little girl we're talking about. Just like you, I never gave up on her all that time she was gone, and I'm certainly not going to give up on her now."

Mom seems to soften then, even as she curls her hands into fists. Then she sighs. "Nothing I can say is going to stop this, is it?"

"I'm sorry, Mom. But no."

She turns to Buck then. "Did you talk her into this nonsense?"

"No, ma'am."

"He did not, Mother. In fact he tried to talk me *out* of it."

"How could he talk you out of it? He's a stranger to you. I'm your mother, little tree. Listen to me."

"And I'm your father," Dad says. "And I won't rest until we see whoever did this to you brought to justice."

Mom sinks her head into her hands, lightly weeping again.

I look down at her, I want to reassure her. I want to sit down next to her and hug her, tell her not to worry. That everything will be all right.

But I don't know that it will be. I don't know that I will come out of this alive.

And I can't lie to her.

"Lisa," Dad says, "you need to be strong. You need to be strong for our little tree."

Mom lifts her head, sniffles, nods. "I can't convince you not to do this, can I?"

"Lisa, you know I love you more than I love the air that I breathe, but no. This is our little girl. Our little tree."

Mom nods then, her jaw going rigid. "Do what you have to do. All of you."

31

BUCK

Monday morning, during a virtual meeting with Reid Wolfe to let him know we're fine, I filled him in on Aspen's wishes.

Whatever you need.

Those were his words.

All the Wolfe resources are at our disposal.

"Wow," Aspen says when I tell her the news.

"Whatever you need. We'll be able to find all the members of your team. Your dad already has the seat records. According to the original seating plan, the person next to you was a player named Margaret Rudolph."

Aspen narrows her eyes. "Margie? No, I would've remembered if she were next to me. She had a body odor problem."

"Maybe she washed that day," I say.

"No... I'm almost sure I would've remembered if it was her."

"Maybe someone changed seats?"

"Maybe. We often did that. Sometimes seats were preassigned, and the taller players, like me, would trade for aisle seats so we could stretch our legs a little better."

"This Margaret? Was she tall?"

"She was...not as tall as I am. But not short either. She was an outdoorsy person, didn't shave, and didn't believe in using chemicals on her body. Hence the BO problem."

"Were you friends?"

"She was a perfectly nice person. No one could really stand to be around her though. For obvious reasons."

"So she wouldn't have anything against you."

"Not that I know of. Then again, I didn't think *anyone* had anything against me."

"The only person to gain from your disappearance was Gloria Delgado."

"I know, but there's just no way Gloria did this."

"Aspen, baby, sometimes you think you know a person, but no one knows what goes on inside another person's head."

She shakes her head adamantly. "No. It absolutely wasn't Gloria."

"You keep saying that, but Gloria had the most to gain."

I don't reply.

"Maybe Gloria's girlfriend then?" Buck says.

"Taylor? I've been over and over this in my mind, and I don't think Taylor could do it."

"Again...you think you know a person..."

"If I had to choose between the two, I'd say it would more likely be Taylor than Gloria, but what would Taylor have to gain?"

"Her girlfriend as the starting middle blocker."

"Gloria never talked about wanting my position."

"She never talked to *you* about wanting your position."

Good point. I'm the one person she *wouldn't* talk to about it. "I suppose that's true."

"Whatever. We'll figure it out. We have resources behind us. The first thing we need to do is talk to Gloria Delgado. I've got an address for her. It's in LA."

"Then I guess we go to LA," Aspen says.

"You sure about this?"

"I'm sure. Even my father agrees."

"Your father is a retired military man. A SEAL, like me. We're wired that way. We're wired never to leave the scene until everything is wrapped up."

"Then you understand."

"Sure. As a SEAL, I understand. As a man? I understand there are sometimes things more important than finding the truth, than revenge. Your mental health for one. Your physical health for another."

"My mental health needs this," Aspen says. "Trust me., I don't want to feel this way, Buck. I really don't. I wish I could be one of those women who just lets bygones be bygones and—"

"Wait a minute. No one is saying you should let bygones be bygones. This isn't the end of a bad relationship. This is someone who betrayed you in the worst way. What I'm saying is that you're alive, you're healthy—at least physically—and to get mentally healthy, you don't need to make this person pay."

"It'll go a long way toward making me mentally healthy," she says.

The SEAL in me agrees with her.

The man? The man who's gone through his own damned therapy because of what he saw overseas?

That man disagrees.

But this is Aspen. This is my forever. I have to be there for her, and I have to support her in this.

"Okay, then."

"When do we leave?"

"Tonight. Six p.m. flight to LA."

Good," she says. "I'll be able to see Katelyn."

IT'S NINE P.M. Pacific time when I drive our new rental car to the Peninsula Hotel in Beverly Hills. The Wolfes said to spare no expense, so I may as well put Aspen up in style. I booked two rooms, of course. I want her to be comfortable. I'm hoping she'll stay with me, but if she chooses not to, I will support that decision.

We had dinner on the plane, and Aspen was surprised when we got first class seats.

"The Wolfes said to spare no expense," I told her.

Her eyes widen when we walk into the ornate lobby of the hotel. "Look at that crystal chandelier!"

"The Wolfes said to spare no expense," I say again.

"That's kind of them. But this is ridiculous. Look at all the marble."

"You deserve the best. They support you wholeheartedly in anything you want to do, baby. They've been good to all of the women."

"They're very kind. How could they..."

"What?"

She shakes her head. "How are they Derek Wolfe's children? I don't understand how one man can be so callous and satanic but have four children who are so amazing."

"There's a lot you don't know about the Wolfes," I say.

"You mean they're not amazing?"

"Oh, they're amazing. It's just they've all been to hell and back as well. They haven't had the easiest lives."

She wrinkles her forehead. "They have all the money they could ever want."

"True enough. But money can't buy everything, Aspen."

"I know. I shouldn't have said that. It was unfeeling."

"You come from a modest background. So do I. I get it. There were times when I was young that I thought if only I had, you know, a hundred thousand bucks to my name, everything would be fine. Doesn't work that way."

"You're right. It doesn't. All the money in the world can't erase what happened to me."

"And there's something else that can't erase it."

She nods. "I know that, Buck. We've been through this... how many times now? I understand that I don't need this to heal. I *want* it."

"I understand."

And I do. I absolutely do.

I just know that, sometimes, getting what you *want* can make things worse.

32

ASPEN

I text Katelyn in the morning with my new phone.
I'm here in LA. Can I see you?
I watch as the three dots move.

I can't believe you left Manhattan without telling anyone! I was so relieved when I heard from Buck that he had found you.

I'm really sorry I worried you. But we're here.

We?

Buck and me. We're here to do some investigation.

On what?

I want to find out who sold me to the island.
Nothing for a few moments. Then—

Are you sure?

*You know who sold *you* out. I just want the same.*

Again, no reply for a few moments. Until—

I understand. Of course I want to see you. How about lunch?

Okay. You pick the place. I don't know anything in LA. I'm at the Peninsula Hotel.

Will do. I'll text you with details. And...do you mind if I bring my fiancé?

My jaw drops. *Fiancé?*

It's a long story. But I can't wait for you to meet him.

Actually...

I don't want to be rude. Katelyn is obviously bubbling with happiness and wants me to meet her man. But I need to talk to Katelyn about other things. Things I don't really want to discuss in front of a stranger.

Then my text dings.

It's okay. I understand. It'll just be us girls.

I heave a sigh of relief.

Thank you. I do want to meet him. But I'm in town for another reason.

A long pause, until—

Are you sure you want to know?

Katelyn knows who sold her out. It was her cousin, and

he's in prison on some unrelated matter. Drugs, I think. But at least he's put away. Katelyn knows he set her up, and she's getting on with her life. Why shouldn't I get on with my life?

I do, I text back. I truly do.

Okay then. Can't wait to see you.

Someone knocks at my door, and I jerk. It's probably just Buck picking me up for breakfast. We were both exhausted last night, and I asked him to sleep in his own room.

I felt kind of bad about it. It's not that I didn't want to be with him, but I knew that if I stayed with him, we'd end up having sex all night. Not that that would've been a bad thing, but I just needed to sleep so I'd have a clear head today.

I promised Buck I would do some soul searching about this whole ordeal. Is it what I truly want? Is it what will be best for me in the long run?

A talk with Katelyn may help me figure that out, but at this point? I'm all in. I want to know who did this to me, who decided they had control over my fate, my life.

Who hated me so much that they would do something so horrendous.

That's how I know it wasn't Gloria. Gloria didn't hate anyone. Gloria was the one who led our moment of silence before and after each game, and she's the one who always had a smile for everyone.

And Taylor? She was also very nice. I didn't know her well —I had only recently joined the team, so I didn't know anyone very well—but Gloria spoke highly of her. She never said a mean word to me that I can recall.

There were a couple of players who were bad seeds. But neither of them were sitting anywhere near me on the plane.

I would've remembered that.

Besides, I know who sat next to me. Dad has the information that he gave to Buck. But again... We changed seats a lot. But no, I know I would remember if one of the bad seeds—Laura or Celeste—had been next to me.

Laura and Celeste were egomaniacs. They were talented, for sure. Everyone on the team was. But Laura and Celeste were vicious as well as talented. Not vicious in a high school kind of way. They didn't pull the usual hazing pranks, but it might have been better if they had. They were worse. They were the kind of people who would smile to your face and then stab you in the back.

They excelled at it.

I stayed out of their way. For the most part they stayed out of mine. As far as I know, they didn't have anything against me other than the fact that they hated all of us.

They were very good players though. I don't think Coach would've put up with them otherwise.

Laura had been accused of domestic violence by her live-in boyfriend. The charges ended up being dropped, though I don't know the details.

But honestly? She probably did it. She was a big girl like me, muscular and tall.

Boy, I haven't given the two of them a thought in I don't know how long.

It's funny. When you get trapped on an island and faced with real evil, mean girls like Laura and Celeste become nothing. Inconsequential.

"You ready for breakfast?" Buck asks.

"Yeah. And then if you don't mind, I'm going to have lunch with Katelyn."

"Why would I mind? It will be nice to see her."

I clear my throat. "You don't understand. I want to have lunch with her alone. I kind of told her she couldn't bring her fiancé."

Buck's eyes widen. "God, don't tell me she got engaged to him."

"Who?"

"Lucifer Ashton. You probably know him as Luke."

"The hottie waiter from The Glass House?"

"The hottie waiter from The Glass House is not what he seems to be. But he does seem to care about Katelyn."

"That's all that matters, isn't it?"

Buck doesn't answer my question. Instead, "Let's go to breakfast."

"Sure." I grab my purse and follow him to the elevator.

It's a buffet again, and I load my plate was scrambled eggs and bacon, while Buck waits in the omelet line. This man loves omelets.

When he gets back to the table, he takes a bite, chews, swallows. "So many days in the field, we had these MRE omelets that made me want to retch."

"MRE?"

"It stands for 'meal, ready to eat.' Vacuum sealed mush is what they really were."

"How can you eat omelets now, then?"

"Because I love omelets. That shit they served us wasn't an omelet. It tasted like speckled brains or something."

I can't help a laugh.

"You're laughing at speckled brains?"

"First of all, brains aren't speckled, at least not that I know of. And second of all, even if they were, how would you know what they taste like?"

He smiles. "I don't know. It's what came into my mind when I had to eat that shit."

"Why did you eat it?"

"In the Navy, you don't ask why. You eat what they fucking give you. If you don't, you go hungry."

"Oh." Of course. The daughter of a Navy SEAL should know that. I mean, how many times did my father stand over me when I refused to finish the last broccoli floret?

You eat what your mother puts in front of you, or you go hungry.

A couple times I went hungry.

My mom was a good cook, but to this day, I still can't stomach broccoli. I'll never eat it again, now that I'm an adult.

"How come you didn't tell me your dad was a Navy SEAL?" Buck asks me. "I can't believe you didn't recognize the SEAL trident on my forearm and the big one on my back."

"I do recognize it. Now. It seemed familiar... It's just... My memory is so screwed up."

"Did you forget your dad was a SEAL?"

"No. I just didn't mention it."

It's not a good answer, and he stares at me as he chews on a slice of bacon. The trident *did* look familiar... My brain is just a mess. I don't put things together like I used to, but it's getting better.

"So what do you want to talk to Katelyn about?" Buck finally asks me.

"Just stuff. I'd like to talk about what she remembers. And of course I want to hear all about how she came to be engaged."

"Has she shared with you anything about what happened to her in the last couple weeks?"

"No. I mean I know she went to LA to see her dad. He had some kind of biopsy on his liver. But since she didn't say anything— Crap, I should've asked how he was doing. I'm being so self-absorbed."

"Her father's fine. His biopsy was benign."

"How do you know that?"

"I get all my information from the Wolfes."

"God, I feel like an asshole for not asking about him."

"You're going through your own stuff. She understands that. She of all people understands that."

Buck is right, of course. Still, I feel bad. I'd like to consider Katelyn a friend. It's funny. I sat with her in that front room of the dorm many times while we were in captivity. She and I and Onyx. Sometimes another girl would join us. But more often than not it was just the three of us watching old *I Love Lucy* reruns.

It was a respite.

We could focus on something other than our horrible circumstances. Still? Some of the girls chose to stay in their rooms. But Katelyn, Onyx, and I sat on the couch together, our eyes glued to the TV. We didn't talk to each other, not about anything important anyway.

We weren't ourselves back then. Katelyn didn't even remember her name. I always remembered mine. No one called me Aspen on the island, only Garnet. But I never let myself forget who I was.

That was the difference between Katelyn and me. She became Moonstone on the island. That was how she protected herself.

I was already able to protect myself better than most of the women, which is why they went after me so viciously.

God, it's too much to think about.

Maybe Buck is right. Maybe it's best to let it all go, to leave it in the past where it belongs. I'm lucky to be alive.

So I forgot the SEAL trident for a minute. I'm lucky I can still think, that my mind still works. Some of the women are still on the island, still at the retreat center, having broken with reality.

I'm one of the lucky ones.

"You're not touching your breakfast," Buck says, interrupting my thoughts.

"Just thinking." I take a sip of coffee.

"About what? Anything you want to talk about?"

"I'm sorry...about last night."

"About not staying in my room with me? Baby, you don't ever have to be sorry for that. I will never ask anything of you."

"I know that. And it's not that I didn't want you."

"I understand."

"I just wanted to think. I thought a lot about what you said, Buck. About whether it's worth it to try to find who's responsible for my situation. But my father is on board, and I just feel like this is something I have to do. It will help me have some closure, you know?"

Buck meets my gaze as he swallows a bite of omelet.

I see something in his dark eyes—something kind and gentle yet determined and willful.

"Whatever you need, Aspen. I'm here for whatever you need."

33

BUCK

Closure.

It's a word therapists use, but it's essentially meaningless. How do you have closure after something so horrific? Do you do it Aspen's way? By finding out who was responsible in the first place?

Or do you do it my way? By trying to move forward and leaving the past in the past?

In truth? Neither leads to closure. Closure is a euphemism for moving on.

Nothing is ever closed. Those things are always part of you. Still, therapists like to throw the word "closure" around like it's a baseball.

And it still means nothing.

It doesn't heal you, and it doesn't take away the pain. The past will always be a part of you.

I feel that Aspen is making a mistake, but I will support her. Whatever she needs.

If it's closure she's after? She'll never find it. No one does, and no one knows that better than I do.

I clear my throat. "So after lunch with Katelyn, how do you want to proceed with Gloria Delgado?"

"Do you have an address for her?"

"A home address, a work address, and a phone number."

"Where does she work?"

"She doesn't play volleyball anymore. She's an assistant coach at West Beverly Hills High School. She also teaches history."

"High school?" Aspen raises her eyebrows. "Not pro or semi-pro? Or at least college?"

"That's the information I have," I say. "I thought it was kind of weird as well. Like a fall from grace or something, but it may be nothing. It may be circumstances and nothing else."

"Maybe..." She sighs. "This afternoon, I guess. I don't want to bother her at work."

"School lets out at three p.m., but then she has volleyball practice after school. She's usually done by four thirty."

"So I guess we meet her there at four thirty."

"At school?"

"I can't call her, Buck. You know that. She may hang up."

"Do you really think she would? If she's the woman you've described to me—the good and sweet woman—she wouldn't hang up on you."

"I don't want to take the chance. I need to speak to her face-to-face. I owe her that much. I also owe it to myself."

Good. My thought process is a little different. If we show up right after she gets off work, she won't have time to think up an alibi. Aspen may be convinced of Gloria's innocence, but I'm not. I never have been.

"Okay then," I say. "We'll wait for her at four thirty at the school. Do you think you'll recognize her?"

"Do you have a recent photograph?"

"I do." I hand my phone to Aspen.

"She hasn't changed much. Her hair is longer now. But she looks good."

"So you recognize her."

"Yes. Do you think she'll recognize me?"

"I don't know, baby. Your face is beautiful and there's not a scar on it."

"I used to wear long hair," Aspen says. "But I probably look the same. Maybe slightly thinner."

"Well." I clear my throat once more. "We'll see how it goes then."

We finish our breakfast in silence.

After breakfast, I escort Aspen back to her room. "Will you be okay here for an hour or two? I want to go workout."

"Workout?"

"Yeah. I work out for couple hours a day when I can."

"May I go with you?"

"Sure, I guess. I'm not sure why I didn't think to ask you."

"I'm an athlete. A professional athlete. Or at least I was. I'm used to hard workouts. And I hate to tell you this, but I got some of the hardest workouts on that damned island. That might be part of what saved me. The constant endorphins. The constant adrenaline. Because even though I was living in hell on earth, I was never so depressed that I thought about giving up."

"I get it." And God, I do. I worked my ass off overseas on all my tours, so much adrenaline was flowing through my system that I probably would've dropped dead otherwise.

Because there's some things you see—some things you see and hear and feel—that you know don't belong in this world. They're pure evil. They belong in hell.

It's the adrenaline that gets you through it.

"I'd love your company," I say. "Let's go."

34

ASPEN

Buck was serious when he said he was going to work out. He worked me harder this morning than I've been worked in a long time. Forty-five minutes on the elliptical, and then free weights until my abs were burning. I'm going to be hurting tomorrow.

I may be a professional athlete, but I'm not a Navy SEAL.

I have a new respect for my father after this workout.

Katelyn texted me earlier with the location of the restaurant, and Buck is driving me now. He pulls up in the parking lot.

"You sure you don't want me to go in with you?"

"I'm sure. This is something I need to do alone. After all, I pretty much told her she couldn't bring her fiancé."

"I understand."

Though I can't read his expression. He almost looks... Something more than concerned. Fearful for my safety? That can't be it, or he wouldn't leave me here.

"What's wrong?" I ask.

"Nothing. I'll be right out here in the car. No more than fifty feet away. You just text if you need me."

"I will."

He looks like he wants to say something else to me. I raise my eyebrows.

But he stays silent.

"I'll be back," I tell him. "And don't worry."

I walk into the restaurant, and I see Katelyn right away at a table in the back. Her blond hair flounces around her shoulders, and she's wearing a plain white T-shirt. She stands, a huge smile on her face.

"Aspen." She embraces me.

The embrace feels a little awkward at first, but then it begins to feel natural.

Funny how my embraces with Buck never felt anything but natural. It was hard for me to be touched at first, once I left the island, because the only kind of touching I experienced during the past five years was abusive.

"The chicken tacos here are great," Katelyn takes a seat.

I sit down across from her at the small table. She's sipping a glass of water.

"The fish tacos are supposed to be spectacular as well," she continues. "But I can't do it."

I nod. Seafood was so plentiful on the island, and it's what we were fed regularly. We got sick of it, but I always remembered my father's stern voice.

You eat it, or you go hungry.

I went hungry a few times as a child, but going hungry wasn't an option on the island. We found that out right away. First, we needed our strength for the hunt.

And second? One woman—Quartz—once refused to eat. She ended up being strapped down and force-fed.

One by one, all the other women were paraded in to watch her.

We learned our lesson well.

Quartz never refused to eat after that.

And Quartz is another of the women who never made it off the island.

We also learned that the women who made trouble disappeared.

God, I don't want to be thinking about this, not while I'm eating with Katelyn.

On her finger sparkles what must be at least a two-carat diamond.

"So you're engaged," I say.

"Yes. To the son of a billionaire no less."

"So not Luke from the restaurant?"

"One and the same, actually. It's a long story."

"I want to hear every bit of it. And then I've got a lot to tell you as well."

"His real name is Lucifer Charles Ashton the third. He doesn't have the best background. In fact he's lucky that he's out walking. He was a— I guess I don't know what he *was* technically. Just really high-up in the LA drug world."

I nod. This much I already know from Buck.

"But he's a recovering alcoholic, and he got an immunity deal from the Feds. Buck knows all about it. He nearly gave his life for me, Aspen." She bites her lower lip. "I was in love with him before then, but after? I knew he was my forever."

Can people really change? I don't ask Katelyn this question. I don't want to put her on the spot or make her doubt her fiancé.

I'm really asking it of myself.

"I want you to meet him. But I totally understand that you just wanted it to be us today."

"Yeah. Thanks for that. I want to meet him as well. But there's some other stuff I want to talk to you about today. About why I'm here."

"To find out who did this to you."

"Yes. I'm pretty sure it was someone on my volleyball team. I want to figure out why. And I want to know who."

Katelyn smiles and sighs. "None of that will change anything."

"You sound just like Buck. I know that, Katelyn. I know it in the deepest recesses of my soul. But I still want to know. I feel like I need to know for closure."

"All right. What can I do to help?"

Before I can answer, our server comes with menus. "I'm so sorry to keep you waiting. Would you like something to drink?"

"Water's fine for me," Katelyn says.

"Yes, water would be great." I smile. Then I open my menu.

"I'll get that right away for you," she says to me.

"Thank you." I glance at my menu.

It's funny. I grew up in Colorado, and there's this great place for fish tacos in downtown Denver. Fish tacos in Colorado? Totally strange, but boy are they delicious.

But now? I don't eat seafood. Still... Part of me wants to try these fish tacos that are spectacular, according to Katelyn's fiancé.

"Chicken tacos for me," Katelyn says. "Luke brought me here a few days ago, raving about everything. He was right about the chicken tacos."

"There's this part of me that wants to try the fish tacos," I say. "I almost feel like... I almost feel like that if I try these fish tacos, and I'm able to stomach them, I can get through anything."

Katelyn smiles. "You know what? You should order them then. The worst thing that can happen is they make you gag, and then you order something else."

Our server returns, and I close my menu. "Fish tacos for me."

"And chicken for me," Katelyn says.

The server sets my water in front of me. "I'll get those right out for you. Did you want to order any appetizers?"

"Nothing for me," Katelyn says.

"Me neither. Thanks."

And for some reason, just ordering fish tacos makes me feel like I can take on the world.

I don't even have to eat the damned things.

"So how can I help you?" Katelyn asks.

"I'm not sure yet. I'm going to go see one of my former teammates this afternoon. She's a teacher at West Beverly Hills high school."

"So she no longer plays?"

"Apparently not. Her name is Gloria Delgado."

"That name sounds familiar to me."

"It's possible I mentioned her when we were on the island."

"No, I don't think that's it. We didn't really talk on the island."

"That's true. She was my backup on the team."

"That doesn't ring a bell. I'm not sure why her name sounds familiar. Maybe it'll come to me."

"Buck has a theory that Gloria might be behind my situation. After all, she had the most to gain. She took my spot on the team."

"But you don't seem to agree with Buck."

"I see his logic for sure. She *did* have the most to gain. But if you knew Gloria... She was so sweet and so nice. A totally devout Catholic."

"What else can you tell me about her?"

"She was a lesbian. She was dating one of the other girls on the team. Taylor Wallace."

"A devout Catholic and a lesbian?"

"Yeah, and she always seemed fine with that. A lot of Catholics don't care about that kind of stuff anymore. They shouldn't, anyway."

"I totally agree. What else can you tell me about her?"

"She was just...nice. The way I put it to Buck was she was the Miss Congeniality of our team."

"I see. So you really don't think it was her even though she had the most to gain."

"Yeah, it would really surprise the hell out of me if it turned out to be her."

"So what makes you think it was a teammate?"

"Because we were headed to New York for a game, and I started feeling sick after we got off the plane at LaGuardia. So sick that I didn't go to dinner that night. I stayed in my room, and the next thing I know..."

"You are in that damned concrete room," Katelyn finishes for me.

"Give the girl a gold star." I smile.

"It's good to see you smiling, Aspen."

Funny. I *have* been smiling a lot the last couple of days.

"Oh my God," Katelyn says.

"What?"

"You've been having sex, haven't you?"

My eyebrows nearly fly off my face. "How did you do that?"

"It's that look. You look exactly the way I felt. It's kind of like you never thought you'd want to have sex again, and then you meet someone— My God, is it Buck?"

Warmth flies to my cheeks.

"You're blushing. It *is* Buck."

"It doesn't mean anything."

"It doesn't have to mean anything. But I can tell you that Buck is a great guy. He protected me... Gosh, I guess there's a lot I have to tell you."

"There sure is. How exactly do you know Buck?"

"I'm sure he told you part of it."

"A little, but how do you know he's such a good guy?"

"You know he was a Navy SEAL right?"

"Of course."

"I told you Luke turned out to be an ex-drug kingpin. Or rather, the right-hand man to a drug kingpin who is now in prison, thanks to Luke and Buck. Anyway, the kingpin had me kidnapped—"

My heart nearly stops. "No... Please don't tell me you were taken again."

Katelyn takes a sip of water. "I was. And I was scared out of my mind, but Buck... Buck helped me."

"What was Buck doing there?"

"He was looking for Luke. He wanted revenge. It's a long story."

"Yeah, he told me. Part of it anyway."

"Anyway, King, the drug kingpin—"

"His name was King?"

"Yeah. Coincidence. His name is actually Kingsford something. Anyway, to get at Luke, King had me taken."

"Oh my God, Katelyn. I'm so sorry."

"It's okay. That's how I met Buck. Buck had gotten captured by King as well when he went looking for Luke. It's because of Buck that I didn't lose hope, and it's also because of..."

"Because of what?"

"You'll never believe this, but it was because of Moonstone."

I raise my eyebrows. "What do you mean?"

"I had to become Moonstone again. I didn't want to, but I had to."

"I get it." And I do. I understand completely. The island was treacherous, and if I could go back in time and change it for all of us, I would in a minute. But for those of us determined to power through, it gave us an endurance—even for me, as a pro athlete—we wouldn't otherwise have. I can't say I'm grateful. Not at all. But the strength is there, for me and for Katelyn, and it's because of what we went through.

"Do you think you can become Garnet again?"

"It's different with me," I say. "Garnet isn't that much different from Aspen. She only looks different. I had to use all my strength, all the moves I learned as a professional athlete. I was never Garnet, not inside. I was always Aspen."

And I'm still Aspen.

I'm just a different Aspen than I was before I was taken.

Old Aspen was naïve.

Aspen now is no longer naïve.

Aspen now understands how evil people can be, and she wants to make sure they pay.

35

BUCK

I squint.

Sure enough, I see him.

Lucifer Raven. He looks a little different now. His hair is no longer dark. It's a sandy blond.

He stands—wearing Levi's and a button-down, his hands shoved into his pockets—near the doorway to the restaurant.

Clearly he's doing the same thing I am. He's keeping watch over his woman.

Damn him to hell.

It's hard to accept that people change. Damned difficult, if you ask me.

The man abused my sister. My little sister. There's not enough forgiveness in the world for that.

But he seems to have shed the feathers of the Raven, gotten clean from his alcohol abuse, and worked a deal with the Feds so he no longer has to be in hiding and he retains immunity from all of his transgressions.

Yeah, having an old man who's worth hundreds of millions of dollars is quite a boon.

Our gazes meet.

He doesn't like me anymore than I like him.

But, if I end up needing his help to figure out who ultimately led to Aspen's abduction, I'll take him up on his offer.

In the meantime, I simply glare at him.

He doesn't walk over, and I don't leave my car to go see him.

Right now, we're just two alpha males protecting our mates.

Then I let out a scoff.

Mates?

Yes, I fell in love with Aspen. But how is this even possible? I haven't felt like this since Amira, and even then, I don't think it was quite this intense.

A little over an hour later, the two women exit the restaurant. Katelyn—who looks vibrant and happy—runs into Luke's arms. He kisses the top of her head.

Then hands shake, and Aspen gives him a hug.

A knife of jealousy spears through my gut.

I do *not* want Lucifer Raven's hands on Aspen.

Aspen gives Katelyn a hug, they talk for a few more seconds, and then she walks towards me and the car. She opens the passenger door and gets in before I can get out to help her. Just as well, I suppose. I don't want to have to talk to Lucifer Raven.

I mean...Luke. Damn.

"Did you have a good time?" I ask.

"I ate fish tacos."

I wrinkle my forehead. "You...what?"

"It's ridiculous, I know. I can't stand the sight of seafood, as you know, but Buck, this place is supposedly known for their fish tacos, and I felt... I don't know. I felt like if I could eat fish tacos, I could accomplish anything. Conquer the world, even!" Her eyes are wide, and her skin is glowing.

She's beautiful. If fish tacos can do this...

"Were they good?"

"Not even slightly. But I ate them, so I know I can do it."

I chuckle. "You're something. Other than eating fish tacos, though, did you have fun?"

"I did. I really did. It was so good to see her."

I clear my throat. "And you met her...Luke."

"Yeah, Luke. Her fiancé. Funny, I thought he had dark hair."

"He dyed it when he was in Manhattan. He was in hiding."

"Yeah, right. Katelyn explained a lot of it. There's a lot of it I still don't get, but that's okay. As long as she's happy."

Right. As long as she's happy.

I purse my lips.

"I was thinking," Aspen continues, "before we go meet Gloria at the school, could we maybe do some sightseeing?"

"I'm from here, but what do you want to see?"

"I don't know. The Hollywood Walk of Fame? Grauman's Chinese Theater? Rodeo Drive?"

"Can you afford anything on Rodeo Drive?"

"Not in this lifetime."

"Then why do you want to go there?"

I'm aware that I'm being a little short with her. I don't mean to be. Except maybe I *do* mean to be. When I saw Lucifer Raven's arms around her...

"I want to go anyway, Buck. I want to say I walked down Rodeo Drive. I want to be like Julia Roberts in *Pretty Woman*."

"They kicked Julia Roberts out," I say.

"Sure, at first they did. I just want to see it. I don't care about five-thousand-dollar handbags and ten-thousand-dollar shoes. But I'd like to say I walked down Rodeo Drive. That I shopped on Rodeo Drive."

"Sure. Whatever." I shove the information into my GPS.

Finding a parking spot on Rodeo Drive? Damned near impossible. I finally squeeze into a tiny one on a side street.

Aspen seems happy. Maybe she'll change her mind. Maybe if she's happy enough, she'll get rid of her need for revenge.

I can only hope.

"It was so great to talk to Katelyn," she says. "I feel like I could really be friends with her."

"There's nothing stopping you from putting down some roots here. The whole world is at your beck and call." Did those words just leave my mouth? I don't want her to put roots down here. I want her in Manhattan. With me. My heart pounds.

She bites her lip. "I suppose so, but I really should go back to Manhattan. Macy's there, and the Wolfes are there."

My heart resumes its normal rhythm. "It's your decision," I say a little more tersely than I mean to.

"What do you think, Buck? Where do you live?"

"I live in Manhattan. I work for the Wolfes."

"Oh."

Is that disappointment I hear in her voice? She just said she had to go back to Manhattan, so is she disappointed that I live there too?

None of this is making any sense to me. Is she truly not feeling the same things I am? Perhaps she isn't. She still has a lot of healing to do. I can't rush her. I can't risk ruining what we may be able to have if I give her the time she needs.

We walk down Rodeo Drive, and I want to grab Aspen's

hand, but I don't. Something stops me. Aspen pauses to look at each window, her eyes wide.

"You can go in if you want to," I say.

"No, that's okay. It's not like I'm actually going to buy anything. I only want to look." She shakes her head. "How do some people pay these prices?"

"How do you even know what they are? No prices are showing in those displays."

"That's my point. You know it's got to be exuberant when nothing has a price tag."

"Price doesn't matter to the people who shop here."

She sighs, and a look of wistfulness passes over her face. God, does she want this kind of stuff?

No, she can't possibly. I met her family. They're down to earth. Her father was a SEAL.

"I want to understand something, Aspen," I say.

"What?" She gazes into the Gucci window.

"Why do you like to do this? Why do you like to look at all the stuff that you don't want or need and that you can't afford anyway?"

She turns, meets my gaze. "There were a few girls on my team who were from money. It's not that I was envious of them so much as I just wanted to experience their lives. Just for a moment."

"Why?"

She doesn't answer right away, and then her eyes widen farther, and her brows nearly jump off her forehead.

And at the same time—

"Money?" I ask. "How much money exactly?"

"My God, Buck, are you thinking what I'm thinking?"

"Most likely. Someone with money could have gotten rid of you very easily."

"But Katelyn... She told me about her cousin who had her kidnapped. He *did* it for the money."

"Right. But we don't have any evidence that the person who sold you out did it for money. They could have done it for your spot on the team, for Gloria."

"Gloria doesn't come from money, though."

"What about her girlfriend? Taylor Wallace?"

Aspen stares at me, and she drops her purse to the ground. She picks it up quickly.

"Baby... Tell me."

"Wallace Leathers. Taylor's an heiress."

"I'll be goddamned." I rake my fingers through my hair. "It's all making sense now."

"Is it, though? We still don't have any evidence."

"No, it's all circumstantial," I agree. "But Taylor was sitting in the aisle seat across from you. She could've easily put something into your drink without you noticing. Especially if you got up to go to the bathroom or something. You would have had to put your Coke on the tray next to you, and Taylor could have easily slid into your seat under the guise of talking to armpits or something, and—"

"No, I wasn't sitting next to Margie. I'd remember that." She chuckles then.

"What's so funny?"

"You called her armpits."

I shake my head. "Not my best moment. Sorry."

"You're right. But it was funny, Buck. The woman stank to high heaven." She gazes into the next window. "But Margie was a really nice girl. Besides, she wasn't next to me. I'd remember."

"We need to figure out who it was," I say, "because if Taylor had money, and the person next to you didn't..."

"Oh my God..."

"This is still all circumstantial," I say. "We'll get more information this afternoon when we talk to Gloria."

"Yes, if she's forthcoming."

"If she's the person you think she is, she will be forthcoming. And if she's not? Well, then we'll know the truth."

36

ASPEN

"That's her," I say.

Gloria Delgado hasn't changed hardly at all. She still wears her black hair long—a bit longer now—although it's pulled into a high ponytail this time. For games, she used to French braid it. She's wearing pink Capri pants and a white button-down, gold flip-flops.

"You recognized her that quickly?" Buck asks.

"Yes. She looks the same. Maybe she's put on a little bit of weight, but she still looks great."

"You want me to go with you?" he asks.

"No. Not yet, anyway. I don't want to scare her off."

"Good enough. I'll be here, and you have your phone."

I nod and click the passenger door side of our car open. I walk briskly toward Gloria.

"Excuse me? Gloria?"

"Do I know you— oh my God! Aspen?" Gloria's hand flies to her mouth.

"It's me."

"It can't be. Everyone said you…"

"Died? Announcements of my death were premature, Gloria."

I drop my gaze to her left hand. She's wearing a gold band. Is she married? To Taylor? Or to someone else?

No, not Taylor. Taylor comes from money. Gloria probably wouldn't be working, or if she were, she'd be doing something a lot more exciting than teaching history at a high school. She'd have a coaching position at some elite university. Or maybe it's always been Gloria's dream to teach high school. I have no idea.

"What are you doing here? What happened to you?"

"It's a long story, Gloria."

"Oh my God," she says. "When the news broke about that island in the South Pacific. Derek Wolfe's Island..."

"So you knew?"

"No, I didn't know. But I had this feeling. I had this feeling that one of those surviving women might be you. The news said one of them was a volleyball player."

"But you didn't look any further?"

"How could I? No one was releasing your names. But I just thought... maybe..."

"You were right on target," I say. "And I wonder, why did you have that feeling?"

"I don't know. It was all long ago. You're so big and so strong, Aspen. I just knew you couldn't be dead."

"I need to talk to you," I say. "I think you might have some information that I need."

"What kind of information would I have?"

"You were my roommate at the hotel when I disappeared. You were one of the last people to see me before I was taken."

"Someone actually came in and took you?"

"How else would I have gotten out of there? But I honestly

don't know, Gloria. I don't have any memories of any of it. I was obviously drugged."

"This is too much." She shakes her head. "I need to get out of here. This is my place of employment, Aspen. I can't talk about this here."

"Come with me then."

Her eyes widen. "Right now?"

"Yes, Gloria. Please."

Her lips tremble.

My God. Is she frightened of me? And if she is... *Was* she behind this all along?

Something hits me like a brick to the head. I need to get her to come with me now. Because if I don't, she will disappear. Call it intuition. Call it a hunch. Call it whatever.

But I'm assured of its truth.

"Please. Have supper with me. We can go now. I need to talk to you."

She looks around, over her shoulder. "Where's your car?"

I nod toward the rental car in the parking lot. "It's right there. I'm with my bodyguard."

She gulps. "Your bodyguard?"

"Yes, he's a former Navy SEAL. He can easily protect both of us, Gloria."

She gulps again. "How about...tomorrow?"

"I'm leaving town late tonight. So it has to be now, Gloria. Please. We were friends once. Do you remember?"

She softens then. "I do remember, Aspen. I do."

"Then please. For old time's sake. For an old friend. Have dinner with me tonight."

37

BUCK

I don't like her stance. Whoever this Gloria Delgado is, she's hiding something. I'm not sure what Aspen is asking her, but it's obviously making her uncomfortable.

And that makes me uncomfortable.

Finally, the two of them head toward the car.

"Great news, Buck," Aspen says when she opens the passenger door. "Gloria has agreed to come to dinner with us."

I hide my surprise. I'm good at that. "That's great," I say. "Hey, Gloria, I'm Buck. Buck Moreno." I unlock the doors to the back seat.

Aspen opens the door for Gloria, and Gloria slides in. She still looks pretty darn timid, like she doesn't want to be here.

Aspen and I will not harm her, and she'll get a free dinner. She can be as scared as she wants to right now, but she'll find out quickly that there's no reason to fear either of us.

"What kind of food do you like to eat, Gloria?" I ask.

"Mexican. American. Italian. Nothing Asian."

"Easy enough to find good Mexican or Italian food here in LA," I say. "You have any favorites?"

She clears her throat. "Whatever you like is fine."

Good. Good answer. For a moment, I was berating myself for asking. She could easily take us somewhere where we may not be safe.

Aspen may be right after all—maybe Gloria had nothing to do with this. She's scared simply because her friend has come back from the dead. Who wouldn't be freaked out to see a ghost?

"Neither of us are from here," Aspen says. "It's early, so we shouldn't have too much trouble getting a table. I'll do a quick search."

While Aspen fiddles with her phone, I drive off the school grounds. My job here is a simple one. I need to make Gloria feel more comfortable in a car with a strange man and a woman she no longer knows.

"How long have you been teaching at West Beverly?" I ask Gloria.

"Only two years. Since I stopped playing volleyball professionally."

"How come you stopped?" Aspen asks.

"I got injured. Plus...I guess I was getting old."

"Are you older than I am?" Aspen asks.

"I'm thirty now."

"Oh. You are a few years older than I am. Funny how we never talked about that on the team."

"I never really felt I had friends on the team," Gloria said.

"Sure you did. You and I were friends. And of course there was Taylor."

I peek in the rearview mirror. Gloria's cheeks turn red. "Right, Taylor. I haven't thought about her in a while."

"I see you're wearing a wedding band," Aspen says. "So you're not married to Taylor?"

"No. She and I didn't last. In fact..." She wrinkles her forehead, clearly thinking. "We broke up soon after you disappeared, Aspen."

"Oh? What happened?" Aspen asks.

"We really didn't have much in common. Other than the team, course."

Interesting. Maybe Aspen's hypothesis is correct. Maybe Taylor *was* behind this, and maybe Gloria knows more than she's letting on. Maybe...Gloria ended a relationship with Taylor over what happened to Aspen.

I'm getting ahead of myself, but it's how my mind works. I take the evidence I have and form it into my hypothesis. You have to think fast, think on your feet, when you're in the trenches.

"I found a place," Aspen says. "Just a mile up the road."

It's not Mexican or American. Maggiani's. Clearly Italian, and the lasagna won't be nearly as good as my mom's.

Parking, of course, is a problem, so I use the valet. What the heck? It's all on the Wolfes anyway.

We go in, and there's a five-minute wait for a table. We find seats on a bench, and we stay silent. We can hardly talk about what we want to talk about in the middle of a crowded entrance of the restaurant.

A few minutes later, we take a seat at our table with the menus our server provides. Gloria, her hands trembling, opens her menu.

"Have you ever been here before Gloria?" Aspen asks.

She shakes her head. "I haven't."

Hmm...strange. Gloria said she likes Italian food, and this place is very close to her place of employment.

The server brings water. "Can I get anything else for you to drink?"

"I'll have a glass of Chianti," Aspen says.

Interesting. She ordered something with alcohol. I'm not sure I've seen her do this.

"Just water for me," I say.

"And you ma'am?" She nods to Gloria.

"Water for me as well."

"Perfect. I'll get that wine for you, and I'll be back to take your dinner orders."

I don't bother looking at the menu. I already know I'm ordering lasagna.

"I think I'll have the chicken piccata," Aspen says.

We both look at Gloria. She stays silent, twisting her lips into a grimace.

"Are you all right, Gloria?" I ask.

"I'm fine. I just need to... Would you excuse me? I need to use the ladies' room."

"Of course." I meet Aspen's gaze, attempting to send her a message with my eyes.

Go with her.

Aspen understands immediately and stands. "You know, I need to go as well. Would you excuse us, Buck?"

"Of course."

I can't blame Gloria for wanting to make a quick getaway. I'd probably do the same thing if I were in her shoes. That's why I sent Aspen after her, to keep her from leaving.

The server returns with Aspen's wine.

"I'll have lasagna, and one of the ladies wants the chicken

piccata. The other hasn't decided yet. They're in the restroom."

"Not a problem. I'll be back in a few." She whisks away.

I take a deep drink of my water and eye the glass of Chianti sitting in Aspen's place.

I sure as hell could use a drink right about now.

38

ASPEN

"Gloria, please," I say once I realize we're the only ones in the bathroom.

"Please what?" She's trying—and failing—to sound nonchalant.

"You're going to leave, aren't you?"

"No, of course not. I just have to go to the bathroom." Her cheeks are red as she makes her way to a stall.

"I'm sorry to have presumed."

I don't dare go into a bathroom stall myself. If I do, she may make a run for it, and I want to make sure she goes back to the table.

Am I making this up? Perhaps, but Buck was thinking the same thing.

I don't hear the tinkle of pee, and if she's as nervous as I think she is, she's most likely got stage fright anyway. She stays in the stall for about five minutes, and then I hear the toilet flush. She comes out, washes her hands, dries them.

All while I stand there.

She knows and I know why we're both here.

"There's no one else in here, Gloria," I say. "You want to tell me what you know now? While it's just the two of us?

"Aspen, I want to help you, I truly do. But I just don't *know* anything."

"We can go back to the table." I stand between Gloria and the door to the bathroom. "You can tell both Buck and me. Or you can tell me. Here."

I don't want to frighten her. At one time we were pretty evenly matched. No longer. I'm in way better shape than she is. Anyone who spent five years being hunted trying to escape degenerate men is in good shape. Way better shape than any volleyball player, and Gloria doesn't even play anymore.

She knows this. I can see it in the look in her face—in her darting eyes and quivering lips. She's not frightened exactly, but she's apprehensive. She doesn't know if she can trust me anymore.

Which is fine. I don't know that I can trust her either, and I *did* trust her at one time. I trusted her more than any other player on that team.

My trust may well have been misplaced.

Or maybe it wasn't. If she's no longer with Taylor...

"What happened with Taylor?" I ask her. "I know it may be painful for you to talk about, but I need to know. I need to know if—"

"Aspen, no! Taylor didn't have anything to do with it!" She clasps her hands to her mouth.

So she *does* know what this is about, and she knows what I suspect.

Is it possible that Miss Congeniality wasn't so congenial after all? Maybe all those prayers were for my disappearance so she could have my position on the team? I shake my head slowly.

"It's not what you think," she hiccups.

"That assumes you know what I'm thinking, Gloria."

"Of course I know what you're thinking. You think I'm behind all of this. Just to get your spot on that stupid team that I couldn't care less about anymore."

I open my mouth to reply when someone walks through the door. She goes to a stall, does her business, returns to the sink, and washes her hands.

Gloria and I say nothing until the woman leaves the bathroom.

"You certainly had the most to gain," I say, keeping my voice low and robotic.

"I know that. I know how this must look. But I swear to God, Aspen, it wasn't me."

"Did you take my spot on the team?"

"Of course I did. That was my job. I was your backup."

"Who else could've gained from you taking my place on the team?"

"Why? Why are you so sure it was a teammate?"

"Because of the timing, Gloria. Even you have to admit that the timing makes sense."

"You got sick."

"Yes, I got sick. I started feeling sick after we landed at LaGuardia. And I was sick enough that I didn't go to dinner. Remember?"

She nods, biting her lower lip.

"Of course you remember," I say. "Because when you got back from dinner, I wasn't there."

"I feel terrible about it. I just thought... I thought you were feeling better and had gone out. I never expected that you wouldn't come back."

"Gloria..."

"How can you even think this of me? I prayed for you at dinner."

"Out loud?"

"No, of course not out loud. I say my prayers silently before I eat. I always thank the Lord for my food. I always ask Him to be there for people who I think need a little help. You weren't feeling well, so I included you in my prayers that evening before I ate."

"And you consciously remember doing that?"

"I don't know. Consciously? Maybe. It's what I do. It's what I always do."

"So you can't say you consciously remember."

"Maybe not specifically. But it's what I do, Aspen. You were ill, so I would've included you in my dinner prayer."

I sigh. She believes what she says. I see it in the sincerity in her eyes.

"Even if you had nothing to do with any of it, I still need to know what you know."

"Please. Just let me go."

"You're not here against your will. You came with me voluntarily."

"I did, but I... I don't know this guy you're with."

"He's my bodyguard. He's paid to keep me safe. You have nothing to fear from him."

"But I—"

"Listen. If you truly had nothing to do with any of this, then you have nothing to fear. Not from Buck and not from me."

She's still quivering, and her jaw is set, as if she's grinding her teeth.

And I know.

God, I know.

Gloria *does* have information for me. I honestly don't believe she was behind it, but she knows who was.

And damn, she's going to tell me.

"I don't want to harm you, Gloria. But you obviously know something, and I will do what*ever* I have to do to get that information."

39

BUCK

Ten minutes pass.

Then fifteen.

When it gets to twenty, I rise.

This has gone on long enough.

I'm not the kind of perv who goes into women's restrooms, but I have a duty to Aspen. I'm here to protect her, and though I don't think she has anything to fear from Gloria Delgado, Gloria could have called someone.

I make my way to the area where the bathrooms are, and I knock on the door to the ladies room. "Aspen? Are you in there?"

A few seconds later a woman comes out. "There's no one else in there, sir."

"Okay. Thanks."

Once the woman is out of my sight, I peek inside the bathroom myself. She wasn't lying. All the stalls are empty, and no one is standing at the sink.

"Damn," I say aloud. I race out of the bathroom and then out of the restaurant. "Aspen!"

Where the hell—

Then I see her. She's on the ground, holding Gloria down. Two cops stand in front of them.

"Fuck," I mutter as I race toward them.

"Ma'am," one of the cops says. "Get up."

"Not until she tells me what I need to know." From Aspen.

"It's okay," Gloria says. "We're friends. I'm not going to file any charges."

"You've got a woman holding you down, miss. Not filing charges is your choice, of course, but we're in the middle of a busy street. You both need to get up."

Aspen finally rises, brushes off her jeans. "I'm sorry." Then she holds out a hand to Gloria, who takes it.

"Are you okay, ma'am?" the other cop asks Gloria.

"Yes, I'm fine."

"You sure you didn't hit your head when you went down?"

"No. I'm absolutely fine. See for yourself." She turns, and though her hair is a bit mussed, there's no evidence of any head trauma.

Thank God.

"I was just scared. Aspen ran after me because she's a friend of mine."

"What scared you, ma'am?"

"Just some stuff from my past. But everything's okay now. Please... You can go."

The cops look at each other. For a moment, I think they're going to slap cuffs on both Gloria and Aspen, but then—

"All right," one of them says. "Here's my card if you change your mind about filing a report." He hands it to Gloria.

"Thank you for your kindness. I won't change my mind."

Once the cops leave— "What the hell was that all about?"

"She tried to run," Aspen says.

"Why, Gloria? Why did you try to run?" I ask.

"I know exactly what you're thinking. I swear it wasn't me."

"Listen," I say. "You were my first suspect when Aspen told me everything, but she swears it wasn't you as well. So if you have nothing to hide, can't you just tell us the truth?"

"It's not that simple."

"She says it wasn't Taylor either," Aspen says, "but I'm not sure I believe her. After all, she and Taylor apparently broke up soon after I was taken."

"I can only tell you this," Gloria says. "If it was Taylor, I didn't know she was involved."

"So you know who was involved then?" I ask.

"Look," Aspen says. "We've got a table at the restaurant. Let's go back in. We can talk."

"Good idea," I agree.

Gloria looks around, over her shoulder, as though she thinks someone may be watching her.

"I'm a professional," I tell her. "If someone were following us, I would know."

She trembles as she nods and accompanies us back into the restaurant.

"Oh good," the host says. "We thought you had run out on the bill."

"The bill? For one glass of wine?" I shake my head.

"I'm afraid we gave your table away," he says. "But I do have another one."

"Fine."

Our new table is closer to the back, which is actually better. Less chance of anyone overhearing us. We take a seat, and the server brings waters. Aspen orders another glass of Chianti, and this time, Gloria joins her.

Probably not a bad idea. Perhaps a bit of alcohol will help her take the edge off. Help her to start talking.

Me? I stick with water.

I want to be on edge right now. I don't want any part of me even slightly inebriated when Gloria tells us what she knows.

"Start talking," I say.

She opens her mouth and then it closes. She does this again, and then three and four times. Our server comes back with the wine.

Gloria takes a sip.

Then she begins to speak.

"I heard a couple of women talking, the day after you disappeared."

"Players on the team?" Aspen asks.

"Yes.

"Who were they?"

"I didn't see who they were, but I know they weren't Taylor, because I know her voice. Or at least I knew it then."

"Laura? Celeste?"

"I can see why you think it might have been them, but I'm pretty sure they had already left the locker room."

"Are you sure?" Aspen asks.

She sighs. "No. I'm not sure. I'm not sure of anything. I didn't see them."

"Wait a minute," Aspen says. "How did you not see them?"

"It was right before the game the next day. I hung back in the locker room to say a quick prayer, since I was taking your spot and I wanted to make sure I was up for it. I also prayed for you, Aspen." She pauses.

Are we supposed to thank her for praying? Is she trying to manipulate Aspen?

Not happening.

Gloria clears her throat and goes on. "I heard two voices coming from the other side of the lockers. Obviously they didn't know I was still there."

"All right. What did they say?"

"One of them just said that *it* was done. And the other said 'when do we get paid?' The first one said, 'the money's already in my account. I'll transfer your half as soon as possible.'"

"Anything else?"

Gloria gulps then. "Yes. The second person said..."

"Go ahead," I say, icicles poking at my neck. "Nothing can surprise us at this point."

Gloria gulps again. "She said, 'dumb bitch got what she deserved. Gloria should've always had that position.' I'm sorry. I hate that word."

Aspen's eyes widen into circles. "So it *was* about you."

"See? You're going to think I was behind it. I swear to God that I wasn't."

"I have never thought you were behind this, Gloria," Aspen says.

"But no one can deny I had the most to gain by your disappearance."

I nod. "Very true."

Aspen glares at me, but I have no remorse. I'm still not convinced Gloria is the sweet little innocent Aspen thinks she is.

"What did you do then? Did you let them know you heard them?"

"Of course not. They didn't know I was listening. And I didn't want to know any more."

"No, you just wanted Aspen's position on the team." I say matter-of-factly.

She bites her lip, and her eyes glaze over.

"Buck..." Aspen admonishes.

"Let's get this straight," I say. "Aspen never thought you had anything to do with this. I've made that clear. But I've seen a lot in my short life, and you know what's pretty remarkable? When it looks like a duck and quacks like a duck, chances are it's a fucking duck."

Gloria cringes at my use of the F-word.

"Buck, please..." From Aspen.

"Look. Unless you can tell us who these people are, and why they had something against Aspen, it sure as hell looks like you're involved."

"I had to wait in the locker room until they left," Gloria says. "I couldn't risk them even thinking that I might've heard them. So I waited. I waited, and when I finally heard them walk out, I waited some more.

"Why?" Aspen asks.

"Because if the two of them saw her coming out right after them, they'd know she might've heard them," I say dryly.

"Yes, exactly," Gloria says.

"Here's the thing," I say. "Would you even be thinking that at the time? If you are who you say you are, and who Aspen thinks you are, why didn't you go straight to the authorities? Or at least to your coach? Why didn't you report these two?"

"How could I report them? I didn't know who they were."

"You didn't have to know who they were to report them," I continue. "All you had to do was go to your coach. Go to the volleyball commission, or whoever governs professional volleyball. Go to whoever would listen. Especially after Aspen didn't return the next day, and then the next."

Gloria stays quiet.

And Aspen finally speaks. "You didn't want me to come back. You wanted my position."

Gloria says nothing more.

"Perhaps you didn't have anything to do with what happened to Aspen," I say, "but by not reporting what you heard, you guaranteed she was never found. So those five years she spent on that island? They're on you, Gloria. They're on you as much as they are on the people who sold her out."

40

ASPEN

I'm frozen. Frozen in time. My veins have turned to ice.

Gloria. The look on her face is contorted, sad, remorseful. Tears well up in her eyes. Her lips tremble, but I'm over it.

I can never forgive her.

"If I could go back," she says. "I would do it all differently."

I say nothing.

Buck says nothing.

"Please believe me. Things are different now. Things changed after that, and that's why Taylor and I broke up."

"How does your breakup with Taylor have anything to do with this?" Buck asks.

"She told me she loved me after that. Told me how proud she was of me that I had the position on the team."

"You guys hadn't said I love you before that?" I ask.

"No. We were kind of just fooling around. I mean, I know I'm very close to my religion, but I never took the adultery thing seriously. And I use birth control."

"Why would you need birth control with Taylor?"

"I didn't. I use it now. With my husband."

"So you switched sides?" I say.

"I never really had a side. I've always considered myself bisexual. And two years ago I met a wonderful man. But we're not ready for kids yet, so I use birth control."

I say nothing.

Buck says nothing.

"Please. If my husband finds out any of this, what will he think?"

"That you didn't report what you heard?" Buck says. "Well, if I were him, I'd—"

I glare at Buck. Then I wonder... Why do I still care about Gloria?

"Gloria," I say, "I *will* find out who did this to me. And you will help me."

"But my marriage..."

"If your marriage is worth saving, it will be saved," Buck says tersely. "If not, it won't be."

"I thought all of this was behind me..." Gloria sniffles.

"It will be behind you when and only when Aspen is able to confront the people who ruined her life." I curl my fingers in a fist, and it takes every ounce of strength I possess not to ram that fist down on the table.

"So you're going to help me," Aspen says firmly.

Gloria sniffles again. "All right. I'll help you. If God can forgive me for what I've done, perhaps Brian can as well."

I ATTACK Buck as soon as we get back to the hotel.

I rip his shirt down the middle, sending buttons flying.

"Baby... My shirt... It's my only one."

"Yeah, and you've been wearing it for days. We'll go shopping. Right now I need you. Please, Buck. Now."

Escape. That's what I want. All those nights I dreamed of escaping that horrible island, but I never was able to escape anywhere but my mind... My escape consisted of blocking out the most horrific memories.

Now though? I can escape into Buck's magnificent body.

"Do you want to talk? I know you think that Gloria—"

I silence him with a kiss.

I shove my tongue into his mouth and kiss him hard.

He returns my kiss. He's a man, after all. Sure, he cares. He gave me the chance to talk if I wanted it.

I didn't want it.

I may never want it again.

I may want to just have sex and fuck and screw his brains out until my own brains are nothing but mush.

Mush for brains.

Sounds great.

When I finally break the kiss so I can inhale a much-needed breath, he starts talking again.

Easy way to fix that. I drop to my knees, unbuckle his belt, unsnap his jeans, and shove them down his hips. His cock springs forward in all its eight-inch decadence.

I take it between my lips.

Yep. That shut him up.

First time I've had a dick in my mouth since— Nope. Not going there.

Stop working, brain.

I take him as far into my mouth as I can. He's huge, but I force it, until he hits the back of my throat.

I no longer have a gag reflex...for reasons which are better left not thought about at this point.

Stop working, brain.

I fuck him with my mouth, hard and fast, the way I want him to fuck me.

I use my fist to increase the pressure, and I suck. I suck him hard.

Soon, he succumbs. He grabs the back of my head, pulling my short hair, moving my head back and forth to his rhythm.

He slows me down a bit, and I'm not surprised. Already I see his balls scrunch up, he's ready to blow.

I resist at first—the hair pulling, him taking control of my movements.

I pull back, and he subdues his efforts.

He understands.

He understands that I need to be in control right now.

Too many times I wasn't in control...

Can't go there right now.

Stop working, brain.

So I continue, but I slow down, taking his lead. I won't get what I want if he blows too soon.

Once he's good and worked up, I pull back, rain a few kisses across the head of his cock.

Then I look into his dark eyes, crane my neck as I still kneel before him.

"God, you look beautiful," he grits out.

"So do you," I breathe.

His button-down shirt still hangs off his shoulders, parted, giving me a glimpse of his bronze and muscled chest.

His hips are firm, and his dick... I never thought I'd

consider that part of a man beautiful again, but I do. On Buck, it's beautiful. Beautiful and majestic and perfect.

"Get undressed," he says roughly.

I rise, shed my clothes in record time.

No longer do my scars and missing nipple humiliate me. No longer do they embarrass me. For what I want from him, I need to be naked, and I need to take charge of my body.

"On the bed," he says.

I obey, and within another minute, I'm lying on my back, my neck and head supported by the pillows, and my legs spread. When I inhale, I can smell my own scent. I'm ripe, wet, so ready for him.

His cock is ready. I was just sucking him, so he's most likely going to thrust inside me quickly.

So maybe I won't have orgasm after orgasm after orgasm, but I will have at least one, and right now I want that dick inside me. Embedded inside me, completing me. Taking away the aching and the emptiness that is so excruciating.

I close my eyes, prepare for the invasion—

Only to feel his velvety tongue swipe across my pussy.

I open my eyes, and his dark gaze meets mine.

"You taste like heaven, baby."

Then he devours me with his tongue, lips, teeth. He scrapes his teeth over my sensitive folds, over my hard little clit.

I wince, but it's not pain I feel. It's pleasure. Intense pleasure.

Then he sucks. He sucks hard. On my clit.

He's doing what I just did to him.

He's taking me to the damned brink, until I can't stand any longer, and then he pulls back.

I lie back, close my eyes again—

"No!"

I pop my eyes open.

"Don't look away from me, baby. Watch me. Watch me eat this delicious pussy."

I have to force myself to watch. My neck wants to roll back, my eyes want to close as I grasp the comforter between my fists.

But I look at him. I stare straight into those beautiful dark eyes, and I do not break the gaze between us. I can't break it, as if we're joined by some kind of electric current.

He eats me. He eats me and eats me and eats me, brings me to the brink and takes me down again, and I clutch at the covers, undulate beneath him, arch my back.

"Buck, please..."

"You're a little cock tease, Aspen. You get what you give." He smiles between my legs.

God. He's driving me slowly insane.

"I guess I can take pity on you." He breaches me with two fingers, finding that spot—

"My God!" I raise my hips as the contractions pulse through me. Everything. Everything in the world has become that glorious place between my legs, that glorious man making it happen.

"That's good," he says. "Come for me, baby. God, you're beautiful Aspen. So fucking beautiful. Do you have any idea how beautiful you are when you come like that? I could watch you all day."

I come down, softly, as if I'm a feather floating to the ground.

When—

He pokes my G spot and sucks my clit, and I'm spiraling upward again.

Up I go, as all the energy in the universe inhabits my body, flows through my cells, in my bloodstream, to my clit.

"There you go, baby. So freaking gorgeous."

Again I begin to flow downward, and again he pushes me higher. Propels me to the top of the highest mountain in Colorado.

Currents spark through me, flames engulf me, and I swear to God my skin is on fire.

It's good fire. The fire that calms my nerves and burns all the horrid out of the world.

For this moment—this one amazing moment—I'm whole.

Whole...and at peace.

41

BUCK

I could eat her forever. Her tart taste, her sweet cries, her beautiful flesh beneath my mouth.

I burrow into her, letting her coat my face, the stubble on my chin, where I know I'll smell her later.

I want her smell surrounding me, a part of me, because...

Because I'm fucking in love with this woman.

I can't even believe it. She's no more ready for love than I am, and it's most likely the farthest thing from her mind. I don't want to scare her, so I must keep these feelings to myself.

But my God, I love Aspen. I love her so damned much.

I continue eating her, throwing myself into her, forcing one more finger into her tight heat.

Three fingers deep now, and she comes again, pulsing around my face.

Everything about her... The scars as well as the beauty. Fuck, they add to her beauty. She is who she is because of the scars, and I love every part of her.

One more orgasm... I'm going to pull one more orgasm out of her before I—

"Buck, no! Please... Can't take it... No more..."

"Yes, you can," I say.

And I massage that G spot with just the right amount of pressure.

She rises, circles her hips, grinds against my face.

And her pussy pulses, those beautiful contractions that slather my face with cream.

Yes, yes. Yes, my love. Come for me.

I munch on her, slide my tongue through those amazing folds, and just when I know she's about to come down—

I climb forward and thrust inside her.

I've come home.

Home at last. Free at last.

Embedded in the woman I love.

No more pain.

No more blood.

No more ghosts of the past.

It's only me. It's only Aspen. Aspen and me. Aspen and me and our love.

Because she will love me back. I'll make it happen. She has to.

I will never let this woman go.

I pull out and thrust back in.

Again, again, again.

Within another moment, I'm releasing...

Releasing into the beauty of this woman, into her heart and into her soul...

I'm alive.

I'm alive as the pleasure and intensity shatters through me.

I'm alive.

For the first time in a long fucking time.

I stay inside her for a timeless moment. Her arms are wrapped around me, her nose buried in my neck.

And then...

A choking sob.

I pull away. "Baby?"

"I'm fine."

"You're crying."

"It's... It's a good cry."

"Are you sure?"

"Yes. I just feel so..."

Complete? Sated? Loved?

I don't volunteer any of those words. She has to come to the conclusion herself.

"So... I don't know."

"But it's a good feeling?"

"God yes, Buck. It's a very good feeling."

I pull her close to me. "I understand." I kiss the top of her head, push her hair out of her eyes.

"I never thought I could feel this way again," Aspen says. "In fact..."

"Yeah?"

"I've *never* felt this way. I never knew it could be like...like this."

"I understand, baby." I kiss her forehead. "God knows I understand."

〜

My phone alarm rings at seven the next morning. I wake up, not sure where I left my phone, and then I remember. It's in the pocket of my jeans which are somewhere on the floor.

The bed seems different as I exit, but I don't give it any thought until I get to my phone and turn off the alarm.

Then I look toward the bed, to see my Aspen—

I gasp.

Aspen's not there.

She's probably just in the other room. I go through the adjoining doors and listen for the shower. "Aspen?"

Already I know.

She's gone.

I grab my phone again. She probably texted me.

But she didn't.

Then my gaze drops to the floor.

Her purse.

Her purse is on the floor.

And her phone is in her purse.

She would not have left without her purse and her phone.

This is unreal.

I'm a fucking Navy SEAL. I am *not* a heavy sleeper. No one could've gotten her out of here without waking me.

I run quickly to the mirror, check my neck. Nope. No syringe marks. I haven't been drugged.

This is impossible.

What could've happened?

I have to call the Wolfes. I have no choice. That certainly doesn't bode well for my security guard abilities.

But they have the resources that I don't.

Or—

Maybe I don't have to call them.

There is someone else I can call.

Someone I never wanted to see again, but someone who promised me anything, and someone who has connections that I don't.

Lucifer Ashton alias Luke Johnson. He'll know what to do.

As much as I hate it, I punch in his number.

"Yeah?" he says into the phone.

"It's Buck. Buck Moreno."

"Yeah, I know who it is."

"You're not going to make this easy on me, are you?"

"I have no desire to make anything hard on you, Buck. What can I do for you?"

"Remember how you said you'd help me if I ever needed it?"

"I do."

"I need it. I need you to help me find Aspen."

"Talk. What the hell happened?"

"She's gone. Disappeared from the damned hotel room. Her purse and phone are here, and I know she wouldn't have gone anywhere without them."

"Where were you?"

"Asleep. In... In the adjoining room."

God, I can't tell him that she was taken right under my nose.

"Did you get in touch with the Wolfe family?"

"I'm hoping I won't have to. If you help me."

"I'll help you."

"Thank you," I say begrudgingly. "And Raven?"

"Luke. I'm Luke now. I won't answer to Raven."

"Right. Luke. Please don't tell Katelyn. I don't want to worry her."

No response.

"Luke?"

"I don't keep anything from Katelyn. I'm sorry."

Fuck. "Fine. Whatever. I—"

I drop the phone as Aspen walks in.

I grip her, pull her to me, and crush my mouth to hers.

42

ASPEN

It's an angry kiss—full of rage and fire.

And I love it.

But...why?

I pull away, my lips stinging.

"Where the fuck were you?" Buck growls.

"I couldn't sleep. I went on a run."

"This early in the fucking morning? Without your phone? This is LA! What were you thinking?"

"I was thinking that I'm a prize athlete and can take care of myself."

"Damn it all to hell, Aspen. If something ever happened to you—" He rakes his fingers through his bed head.

"Nothing's going to happen to me, Buck. I'm pre-disastered at this point."

"What the hell is that supposed to mean?"

"All the shit that's gone on in my life? All the shit that's like a one in a million chance? No way does lightning strikes twice in the same spot."

"That's crap. I've seen lightning strike twice in the same spot more than I care to say. More than I care to remember."

"You mean during your tours?"

"Absolutely."

"I'm sorry. I'm so sorry for everything you've been through. But we're not in Afghanistan. We're not in Iraq."

"There's plenty of fucking crime in LA, Aspen."

"Yes, I realize that. But I can take care of myself. I'm bigger than most men."

"I don't give a shit how fucking strong you are. You can't fight a loaded gun."

He's right, of course. I shouldn't have gone out alone, and I shouldn't have gone without my phone.

It's just that—

"I had a nightmare. I couldn't sleep. I tried snuggling up to you. I tried everything."

"Except waking me up."

"I didn't want to disturb you. This has all been hard on you."

"Not as hard as it's been on you, baby. You wake me up at any time for any reason. You got that?" He pulls me to him once more, smashes his mouth to mine.

I open instantly for a primal kiss. He's naked except for his boxer briefs.

He's right. I shouldn't have gone out alone.

But God, I need my life back. I refuse to go around being scared.

I lean into his kiss, grab one of his hands, and shove it under the waistband of my joggers.

He slides his finger inside me.

He breaks away. "Damn, baby. How can you be so wet already?"

I have no response for him. It's amazing that I can get wet at all after what I've been through, but even before, I was never this turned on by anyone. Not Brandon or anyone else.

He drags me toward the bed, throws me down face first. Yanks my joggers over my hips, and then he's inside me.

Fucking me hard and fast.

I don't care about an orgasm. I don't care about anything in this world right now except for his cock inside me.

He grunts, slapping against me, groaning and growling. "Never again, baby. You never fucking leave me again."

Thrust. Thrust. Thrust.

Then a low groan as he releases, and so in tune am I with him that I feel each contraction of his cock as he empties himself inside me.

I close my eyes, slide into the comfort of rumpled bed linens.

He stays on top of me for a while, and I relish the weight of him, his protection, his warmth.

We stay there for a few moments. He keeps me from moving, but I don't feel violated. I don't feel frightened. I feel...enveloped in warmth and soul-nourishing comfort.

His hot breath against my neck... His vibrating groans in my ear...

It's all so comforting, all so—

Bam!

Someone pounds at the door.

Buck jerks off me, pulls up his boxer briefs. "What the fuck?" He races to the door. "Who the hell is out there?"

"Buck? It's me. Luke."

"Oh, fuck. Hold on."

Buck stumbles into his jeans as I secure my joggers around my waist. He opens the door.

Luke Johnson stands there, his blond hair covered in a Lakers cap. He casts a gaze around the room...at me. "I see you found her."

"Yeah. She was out on a jog."

Luke's gaze zeroes in on the phone lying on the floor. "Next time, let me know?"

"Fuck, man."

"What's he talking about?" I ask Buck.

"Your boyfriend here—"

My jaw drops.

"—was on the phone with me, telling me you'd disappeared. Asking for my help. We got cut off in the middle of our conversation."

"She returned. Came back." Buck threads his fingers through his hair.

"Yeah. What the hell was I supposed to think? You claimed she was taken in the middle of the night while you slept in the other room. So when you stopped talking, what the hell did you think would go through my head?"

"I'm sorry," I say. "You must've thought someone attacked Buck."

"Really?" Buck says. "Don't you think you would've heard jostling or fighting or me cussing someone out who came in to do anything to me?"

"Chill, okay? All I knew was that your woman was missing. Then all of a sudden you were gone. I did what I had to do."

"Which was run over here and pound on my fucking door?"

"Damn right. I'm in this now. I'm in this for Katelyn. If anything happened to you"—he gestures to me—"she'd lose it."

"Well, as you can see, we're fine. So you can go."

"Buck," I say, "we should thank him."

"For what? Interrupting us?"

"For being so concerned. About me. About you."

Buck grits his teeth. "Fine. Thanks."

Luke rolls his eyes. "Don't mention it."

"Believe me. I won't."

"I know what we should do," I say. "Why don't the four of us have dinner tonight?"

Both Buck and Luke look at me with arrows flying from their eyes.

"I can see you're excited about the idea. I'll call Katelyn and set it all up."

Their scowls turn into growls.

"Good. That's great. I'm glad you're happy about the idea." I text Katelyn quickly.

"Aspen..." From Buck.

"Look. Katelyn is the closest thing I have to a friend right now, and she would probably say the same about me. So that means you two need to get along."

Oh my God. Did I just refer to Buck, in a roundabout way, as my boyfriend? Significant other? Fuck buddy?

Well, the latter is at least the truth.

Buck meets my gaze.

"I'm sorry, I didn't mean to imply...anything."

"No worries. I guess we're having dinner together."

"I guess so," Luke says. "I'll be heading out. The next time you ask me for help—"

Buck closes the door before Luke can finish.

"That was a little rude," I say.

"The guy's a criminal."

"Reformed criminal."

"We got thrown together a couple of times, but I'll always remember him as the person who hurt my sister."

I'm not sure what to say to that, so I say nothing. I don't have any siblings, so I don't know exactly how Buck is feeling, but I imagine I'd probably feel the same way.

"Katelyn loves him," I say.

"Yes, I know, and you love Katelyn."

"I do. She's my... I don't know. My person."

"You've been watching too much *Grey's Anatomy*."

"I haven't been watching anything. On that stupid island all we could watch were 1950s sitcoms."

He comes toward me then cups my cheek, "God, baby, I'm sorry."

"It's okay. I should let you off the hook. I remember the reference from *Grey's Anatomy* from years ago. But it describes how I feel about Katelyn."

He simply nods. "For you, I will put aside my feelings about Lucifer Raven...er...Luke."

"Thank you."

"There something else I need to tell you, baby."

"Of course. What is it?"

43

BUCK

I love you.

The words are lodged in my larynx, and I want so much to say them to her.

Deep inside, I know she's not ready to hear them, and there's a big part of me that isn't ready to say them yet either.

Even though I'm certain of their truth.

"Buck?"

"It's just... You mean something to me, Aspen. More than just someone I'm protecting."

She touches my cheek, trails a finger over my lower lip. "You mean something to me too. You're more than a body-guard to me." She steps on her tiptoes and brushes her lips across mine.

Perfect.

We'll leave it at that for now. She feels something for me. Perhaps it's not love, but it's something. And that's enough. For now.

"You're my comfort," she continues. "I feel safe with you."

Comfort?

I want to be her comfort. But is she feeling like I'm some kind of father figure?

No. Course not. She's letting me fuck.

God, get out of your own head, Buck.

I kiss her forehead. "I'm glad."

Good. Leave it at that. *But for God's sake, don't say anything more*, I beg her silently.

She doesn't, thank God.

Her phone dings. "Oh! Katelyn thinks dinner is a great idea. In fact, she invited us to their place."

Their place?"

"Apparently, Luke has a house on the beach."

I resist an eye roll. Of course he does. It's the same place—

"What time, Buck?"

"I don't know. Six?"

"Perfect." She taps on her phone. "Six it is. We should pick up a bottle of wine to take."

"I don't know what kind of wine they like."

She bites her lip. "Actually... Let's not. Luke is a recovering alcoholic."

"Yeah. That's right. What if the rest of us want to drink?"

"I'm sure they'll have something. But I don't want to trigger him."

"God, of course not." Sarcasm drips from my voice. "We wouldn't want to trigger him."

"I'm surprised at you," she says. "I get the history. I do. But getting off the alcohol is a big part of what changed Luke."

"You're right, baby. I'm sorry." And I am, as much as I can be. Luke Johnson—or whatever his name du jour is—and I will never be friends. But if I want a future with Aspen, which I do, Luke comes along with it.

"Why don't we take them something else instead?" I offer.

"Like what?"

"I don't know. Tell her we'll bring dessert. We can pick something up at a bakery."

"That's a great idea." She taps on her phone. "Dessert it is."

Is this what it's like to be part of a couple with Aspen? I like it.

Of course, I wish we were having dinner with someone other than Lucifer Raven.

"I'm going to take a shower, baby."

Aspen smiles. "Would you like company?

God, I'm already hard for her again.

"Always."

DRIVING through the ritzy beachfront properties, one of which is owned by Luke Johnson, doesn't sit well with me.

"Here it is," Aspen says.

I drive up into the circular driveway.

And behold a mansion beach house.

Off white stucco with those curved terra cotta roofing tiles. What are they called? Mission tiles? I don't know and I don't care. The house is sprawling, with stucco archways, wrought iron gates, and a fountain—and we haven't gotten out of the car yet.

Damn. This is where he kept Emily secluded. How can I even go in there?

Aspen takes my hand. "It's okay. It's just a house."

I draw in a deep breath. God knows I've faced worse than this.

Much worse.

Still, I feel like I'm heading into rival territory. Like I need to duck and cover, watch for enemy fire...

"You can't stay in the car forever, Buck." Aspen takes my hand.

I draw in another breath and open the driver side door.

I stand.

And I regard the house.

It's adobe brick, and it's massive. It sits on its own private beach on a couple acres.

Movie stars probably live in this neighborhood.

"Come on." Aspen takes my hand. In her other hand, she carries the bag from the bakery containing the raspberry and vanilla torte we picked up.

Raspberry and vanilla torte.

Could anything be more pretentious? Only if we added rose water and saffron.

I allow her to lead me up the cobblestone pathway to the giant stucco Spanish architecture inspired house on the beach.

"Ready?"

I simply nod.

She rings the doorbell, and Katelyn answers, opening the door, a dog—he's gorgeous with one blue and one brown eye —panting at her legs.

"Go on, Jed." Katelyn scratches the dogs head, and he trots away obediently.

Katelyn looks good. Her cheeks are flushed, and her blond hair is pulled back into a high ponytail. She's wearing a light blue sundress that matches her eyes.

And she looks...happy.

Radiantly happy.

Because of the man who hurt my sister.

Yes, I suppose people can change.

I've heard the whole story. I know what Luke went through for Katelyn, to protect her.

"Come on in!" Katelyn grabs Aspen into a hug.

Once they're done embracing, Aspen hands her the bag. "I hope you like raspberry torte."

"I'm sure it will be delicious." Katelyn turns to me. "Hi there, Buck."

I clear my throat. "Katelyn."

As far as I know, Katelyn knows everything. Everything about Luke and what he did to my sister and others. About his past as a drug lord in the LA underground.

About Lucifer Raven.

"It's so good to have you here." She pulls me into a hug.

This is a good woman. A lovely, good woman who's been through much the same as my Aspen has. If Luke makes her happy...

I want to pull away, but I don't want to offend her or Aspen.

So I wait until Katelyn pulls away.

"Luke's out back. He's got the grill going. We're going to have simple hamburgers. He suggested something like filet mignon or Cornish game hens, but I just felt like plain old burgers. I hope that's okay."

"Of course," Aspen says, "as long as it's not anything from the sea. The fish tacos the other day were enough for a while."

Katelyn shudders slightly. "Yeah, I still can't touch the stuff. And it's strange. I grew up here in LA. I grew up on fish and shellfish."

"Maybe someday," Aspen says.

"Burgers sound great," I say dryly.

Katelyn and Aspen exchange a glance.

That's code—not so subtle code—for me to get over myself and try to enjoy my evening.

"Let's go outside," Katelyn says.

"So he goes solely by Luke now?" I say.

"Yeah. He's always hated the name Lucifer, and his family calls him Trey, for Lucifer the third. He's not a fan of that either. So he's Luke now, except from his mom, who calls him Lucy." Katelyn giggles a bit. "He totally hates it, but he's got a real soft spot for his mom."

Lucy. I hold back a scoff. What would he do if I called him Lucy? But I'll behave myself.

"What about his last name?" I ask.

"He wanted to keep Johnson, but his father talked him into taking Ashton back."

I don't respond.

We head through the large house, which includes a foyer, a huge living area with a grand piano—does anyone even play the damned thing?—a dining area off to the side fit for royalty, and then a massive kitchen and family room. Finally we get to the French doors leading outside to a giant redwood deck, and then, about a hundred feet away, the goddamned Pacific Ocean.

I sigh as I walk out.

Will I ever own a house like this? The Wolfes pay me pretty well. Damned well actually, but not enough to afford this kind of house.

No, this is old money. Ashton money that's been around for at least a century. Lucifer Junior, Luke's father, is a B-movie producer. He does okay, probably rakes in a million or two a year, but not enough to set his son up in a house like this.

All of Luke's drug money was confiscated by the Feds, so this is Ashton money. An Ashton house.

The house where he—

"Buck," Aspen says.

"Yeah?"

"I know this is difficult for you," she whispers, "but please... For me."

Damn, those are fighting words.

44

ASPEN

Something niggles at me all through dinner. I smile and talk and eat my hamburger, but something feels off. Not with Luke or Katelyn, or even with Buck, even though it's clear he'd rather be just about anywhere other than Luke's house.

I can't quite put my finger on what it is, so I ignore it as I tell Katelyn and Luke about Gloria and our meeting with her.

"That's great that Gloria's going to help you," Katelyn says.

Buck hasn't said much all evening, though he has put away three burgers, two helpings of potato salad, and three helpings of baked beans.

Not sure I want to sleep with him tonight.

"Something still doesn't sit well with me," I say. "She claims she didn't know anything about it—about my abduction—but something just doesn't feel right. Especially now that we know about the conversation she overheard in the locker room."

"You need to trust your instincts," Buck says.

I raise my eyebrows. "He speaks!"

"What's that supposed to mean?"

"So far all you've done tonight is feed your face," I say.

That gets a laugh out of Katelyn and, to my surprise, out of Luke as well.

Buck shoots flaming darts with his eyes.

I sympathize. I truly do. It can't be easy having to make nice with the man who wronged his sister. And he's doing this for me. I won't forget that.

"Not true."

"I'm really glad you're here, Buck." This from Katelyn, who's feeding Jed scraps from her plate.

Buck softens a bit. He clearly has a soft spot for Katelyn, and I understand why. She's a strong woman, but her blond beauty and fair skin connote a kind of fragility. She's *not* fragile. Not by any means. Her looks totally deceive.

Buck clears his throat. "I'm pretty sure Luke will agree with me on this. Trust your instincts."

Luke nods. "I do agree. Wholeheartedly."

"On my tours, I learned to depend on my instincts, and very rarely did they let me down."

"What do you mean by that?" I ask.

"When you're in a situation where you're going to be killed either way, you have to make a choice. You either walk into a fire or walk into water with a freaking concrete block strapped to yourself. Which choice do you make? You're going to die either way, so you have to depend on your instincts. Your instinct will tell you which path to take. Follow it. That's what I did, and even though I walked into fire many times, I came out alive. I owe that to my instinct."

"You're using fire as a metaphor, right?" I swallow down the image of Buck actually being consumed by a fire.

"In the general sense, yes. Though there was one time when I literally did walk into fire."

"But you don't have any—" I stop.

"I don't have any burn scars? I have a few. I've had some surgeries to make them less noticeable. But I didn't say I stayed in the fire long."

"It's true," Luke agrees. "Your instincts will save you more often than not. I'm not saying it's a guarantee. Nothing is."

I twist my lips. "So you're saying I shouldn't trust Gloria, then."

"I'm saying," Luke says, "if something is telling you not to, don't."

"You don't think it's just me being paranoid?"

"Paranoia can be useful," Luke says. "I'm not talking about true psychological paranoia. Like a paranoid disorder. But when you have a feeling—a gut feeling—don't ignore it."

Something about his words triggers what I'm feeling. What's off. It's Gloria, but it's not what she told us. It's *her*. Something is wrong.

"Oh my God," I say. "I feel like..."

"What?" Buck says.

"We need to go over there. We need to go to Gloria's house."

"Right now?"

"Yeah. I just have a really bad feeling."

"How bad?"

My skin prickles. "I don't know. I feel like we need to confront her, like she's up to something. Maybe she's trying to get out of town."

"She's married, has a husband. You told me yourself that he doesn't know about any of this. My guess is she won't try anything. Because to do so she would have to tell her husband what's going on."

Still, an invisible rodent gnaws at my gut. Something's wrong.

"You told me to trust my instincts," I say.

"Yes, if you feel like we need to go over there right now, I'll take you myself."

I settle down a bit then. I'm just being paranoid. She said she would help, and I have no reason to distrust her.

Except I *do* have a reason to distrust her. She overheard those two players talking, and she didn't report it.

But no one would've found me. No one found any of us until Derek Wolfe was murdered and the truth finally came out about his island.

They had enough money and enough people on the payroll to keep it totally secret.

Nothing would've changed.

Gloria is fine. This is nothing.

"I'm fine. We don't need to go over there."

"Are you sure?" Buck says. "Because I'll take you right now."

"No. Let's have some dessert." And I force the invisible rat inside me to stop chewing at my insides.

BY THE NEXT MORNING, though, I still can't shake the feeling about Gloria. I jostle Buck awake.

"I need to borrow the car," I say.

"What for?"

"I'm going to Gloria's school, just to make sure she's okay."

"All right."

"You're the one who told me to trust my instinct."

"I am. Give me a minute and I'll take you."

The minute turns into half an hour, because Buck showers first.

By the time we get to the high school where Gloria works, it's ten a.m., and the school day has been going on for two and a half hours.

We walk in, and we have to put our bags through a metal detector and walk through one ourselves.

Since when did schools become like airports?

So much happened during the time I was gone.

We walk to the office where a secretary greets us.

"I'll need you to sign in. What are you here for today? Do you need to see your son or daughter?"

"We're not parents," I say. "We're here to see a friend of mine. Gloria Delgado. She's a teacher."

The secretary's eyes open wide. "You're here to see Gloria?"

"Yes."

"Maybe you can help us out then. Gloria didn't show up for work this morning."

"Oh no. Is she sick?"

"Tell me and we'll both know. She didn't call in, which is very unlike her."

The invisible beast gnaws at my gut again. Maybe my instincts were right last night. And if they were...

But I didn't want to look like the paranoid torture victim. I wanted to convince Buck, Katelyn, Luke—maybe most of all myself—that I was okay.

"Have you called her?" I ask.

"Yes, several times. She's not answering, and neither is her husband, who is her emergency contact."

I knew it. Damn it. I knew it. They left town.

"Is there anything you can tell us?" Buck asks. "She and my wife are old friends."

I jerk slightly at his term of wife. But I get it. It makes us look more legit.

"I wish I could, sir. We're all concerned. This is totally not like her."

"Could you call us if you hear from her?" I ask.

"I'm sorry, ma'am. That's not our policy. All I have is your word that you and your husband are friends of hers."

I nod. "All right. I understand."

But Buck pulls a card out of his pocket and slides it in front of the secretary. "I'll take it as a personal favor if you might. Here's a card in case you change your mind." Then he smiles—a dazzling and flirtatious smile.

And I know. If any information comes up, this woman will call Buck.

"I'll see what I can do," she says.

But already I know we won't be hearing from her. Not because she can resist Buck. I mean, who can?

Because Gloria will not be calling. Gloria will not be returning to the school.

Gloria has gone on the run with her husband.

We walk out of the building. "Oh, Buck, we should've gone over last night."

"They might've been gone by then."

"What if they weren't? What if..."

"We made a decision at the time. You can't second-guess yourself, baby. Trust me. It doesn't lead to anything good."

"What do we do now?"

"First thing we do is go over to their place and look for clues."

"How can we do that? It's probably locked up."

"Baby, I was in the military. I've broken into way harder places than some teacher's house."

"But what if... What if we get caught?"

"I've never gotten caught in my life."

"I'm not sure we should. It's a total invasion of her privacy."

"It is, and if you feel that strongly about it, we won't do it. But if you want clues about where she may have gone so we can find her, that's the only way."

He's right. "Okay. Besides, she's not on my side. She never was."

45

BUCK

Gloria Delgado and her husband, Brian Hansen, live in a modest ranch home just outside LA. It's a cookie-cutter neighborhood, all the houses look the same, but the stucco is painted different colors. Gloria's house is a mint green, unusual in LA. A Ford Focus is parked in the driveway.

Of course that doesn't mean anything. They most likely have two cars, and they took the other one when they fled.

If they fled, which it appears they probably did, Aspen was right all along. Gloria knows much more than she's admitting.

I should've followed my instinct as well. Gloria fleeing from the restaurant the other day was a huge red flag.

I've been a little off my game since I met Aspen. She consumes my thoughts, but if I truly want to help her, I need to be all in. I need to have all my senses on high alert.

I park the car in the street, grab the small kit I brought, and Aspen and I get out.

I can't help but stare at her. She's wearing shorts today.

Denim Daisy Dukes, and her legs go on forever. Scars and all, her legs are gorgeous—especially when they're wrapped around me.

Wearing shorts is a big step for her. I need to support her, rather than have my tongue hanging out my mouth like a horny teenager.

She leads me up the concrete pathway to the door. The first thing I notice is there's no screen door. Not odd, since it's so hot in LA they probably keep the door shut and the air-conditioning on.

Aspen knocks.

Then knocks again.

I unzip my canvas kit and reach for my lock picking tools, but before I can do anything, Aspen grasps the doorknob, twists it, and to both of our surprises, it opens.

Then I let my instinct take over.

I pull some blue nitrile gloves from the kit and hand a pair to Aspen. "Put these on."

"Why?"

"Because we don't know what we're going to find in here, and I don't want our fingerprints all over the place."

"But I just opened the door!"

"I know." I grab a red bandana from my bag and wipe the doorknob clean. "Now you didn't."

We walk inside quietly. My shoulder holster digs into my back. I didn't tell Aspen, but I'm armed. I had the Glock delivered when we arrived in LA. I couldn't take my own on the plane, not without checking a bag, and even then it's ill advised. While she was whining at me for taking too long in the shower, I was putting the pistol in place and buttoning up a shirt so she wouldn't notice it.

God willing I won't have to use it.

But something is not right here. Something is not right at all. I suppose they could've left town in a hurry and forgot to lock the door, but that seems unlikely.

"Gloria?" Aspen calls.

"They're not here," I say.

But then I jerk toward a yappy sound.

We walk to the back of the house to find a small dog barking at the back door, which also isn't locked.

"It's a miniature schnauzer." I open the door to let the dog in. He yelps at me for a moment but then runs to a bowl of water in the corner and begins thirstily drinking.

"They left their dog here? Outside?" I shake my head. "These aren't good people, Aspen."

"Oh my God." Aspen walks to the puppy sipping water. She leans down and pets him. "You poor thing. How long have you been out there all alone?"

The dog is too busy lapping water to notice a stranger is petting him.

She fingers his collar, his tags. "Your name is Edgar. Hey Edgar. Are you hungry? Where does Gloria keep your food?"

Aspen rises and begins looking through the kitchen, opening doors, drawers, and cupboards. Finally she finds a few cans of dog food. She pulls one out, opens the flip top can, and pours some of the dog food into Edgar's bowl.

"Come here, Edgar. Are you hungry?"

Edgar is hungry. He gobbles down the food.

"You may have given him too much," I say. "He's a small dog."

"You're right. But who knows when he last ate?"

Once Edgar finishes his food, he goes back to the water and laps up what's left of it. Then he walks slowly toward Aspen. He's made a friend for life, because Aspen fed him.

"I can't believe she would leave her dog," Aspen says. "How could I have been so wrong about the kind of person she is?"

"You're not the first person to misjudge someone," I say. "Don't beat yourself up about it."

Edgar walks out of the kitchen, and then—

His shrill bark echoes throughout the entire house.

"What could he possibly be barking at?" I ask.

"I don't know."

I follow the sound. "Edgar? What's wrong, Edgar?"

I find him in a bedroom, and—

"Oh my God," I groan, as my body goes numb.

I've seen worse. A lot worse, but Aspen's right behind me.

I pick up Edgar, leave the room, and thrust him into Aspen's arms. "Go. Now."

"What is it?" Aspen's lips tremble. "Let me go in."

"Baby, you've seen enough in your life. Do *not* go in that room." I push her out to the hallway and close the door, leaving her and Edgar outside the room.

Edgar was barking at two people.

Gloria Delgado and a man I presume to be her husband, Brian Hansen.

They're both lying in their queen-sized bed, their throats slit.

The bedding is soaked with blood.

Nausea clogs my throat.

I'll never get used to death. I saw it every day for years, and though I no longer double over and lose the contents of my stomach, I still feel sick. So fucking sick.

Of death.

I scan the room quickly for evidence of a struggle, but

nothing is askew. No lamps have been knocked over, and no walls have been dented.

Either Gloria and Brian were attacked while they slept...

Or they were attacked by someone they knew.

I can rule out them being attacked while they slept because Edgar would've woken them up. Unless he sleeps outside, though the dog bed in the corner of the room seems to negate that.

So it was someone known to Gloria and her husband. Someone they trusted, someone who was perhaps staying with them and entered their room while they slept.

But more likely? It was someone they knew, who they let into their home. Who then drugged them, put them in bed, and slit their throats.

I can't let Aspen see this.

She knocks on the door. "Buck. Please. You're scaring me. Please come out."

I unlock the door, open it, and then close it quickly behind me.

Aspen stands, still holding onto Edgar, who's trying to squirm out of her grasp.

"Tell me," she begs. "Please. I can't stand not knowing."

"I'll tell you, but I don't want you going in there."

"You can't stop me!" She puts Edgar down and he scrambles away, and then she walks past me and opens the door.

I grab her before she can go in.

"Don't. You'll thank me later."

"You can't treat me like this, Buck. I'm not that fragile."

"You're not fragile at all, baby. You're the strongest woman I know. But please. Let me protect you from this."

She squirms. "I don't need your protection. Let go of me!"

Edgar comes racing back then and runs into the bedroom, barking.

"Please, Buck... You're hurting me."

That's all it takes. I let her go, and Aspen brushes past me. I don't hold her back.

Perhaps I can't protect her from this. Perhaps she doesn't need to be protected from this.

I walk in behind her. Edgar has jumped up on the bed and is licking the wound at Gloria's throat.

The blood is beginning to clot. Both bodies are gray, and Brian—who's much fairer than Gloria—is starting to look yellow.

They've been dead for a while now.

Aspen runs out of the room and retches in the hallway.

I go to her quickly, hold her. "I'm sorry, baby. I'm so fucking sorry."

She melts against me, says nothing, hiccups quietly, but she does not cry.

"It's okay, baby." I smooth her hair, kiss the top of her head. "It's going to be okay. I promise you."

How can I make such a promise?

I don't know, but with everything in me I will keep that promise. I will keep Aspen safe.

"We should've gone last night," I sniffle into Buck's shoulder. "We should've called last night."

"We couldn't stop this, baby."

"How can you say that? What if—"

"Shhh... We couldn't have. Whoever did this was someone they knew. Look around. There's no sign of a struggle. Nothing is out of place at all."

"So you're saying..."

"I'm so sorry."

"But why? Why would—" I clasp my hand to my mouth. "Someone they knew. Which means this person they knew, possibly a friend, knew she'd been talking to me."

"We can't assume that."

"Buck, don't patronize me."

He kisses the top of my head. "I'm sorry. You're exactly right. This was probably someone they knew, and it probably has something to do with you. Unless they were involved in something else that's awful, which is certainly possible in LA."

"But—"

"Nothing could've prevented this, Aspen."

"She was a teacher, a coach, an athlete..."

"Yes, she was. But that's all you really know about her. The person you knew six years ago probably doesn't exist anymore. Look at how much you've changed."

"But I had a reason to change. I was held against my will, forced to submit to horrific acts with strangers. I can't possibly be the same person."

"We don't know what she's been through in the last six years."

"She didn't deserve this."

"We don't know that."

She pulls back from me then. "How can you say that? No one deserves to die like this."

"Most people don't. I can think of a few who do."

I keep my mouth shut then. He's right. The people who abused me on that island—I wouldn't mind seeing them dead in a pool of their own blood. And I can't even imagine the horrors that Buck has witnessed.

But Gloria is not in the same category as those people. Those people can't even be defined as people.

I cast my gaze around the room. Buck is right. Nothing seems out of place. I've never been in this room before, but wouldn't we see some signs of struggle?

Unless...

"What if someone came in while they were sleeping, injected them with something and then went for their throats?"

"Edgar would've alerted them."

"But Edgar was outside."

"He clearly doesn't sleep outside." He points to the blue fleece dog bed in the corner of the room.

"Right. Maybe one of them got up and let him out."

"Then they would've been up. Whoever came in, they didn't see them or hear them."

He's right, of course. I know what I'm saying makes no sense.

I just want to believe—for a moment—that my ordeal on that island is over.

But it's not over. I'm not allowing it to be over. As long as I'm bent on discovering who did this to me, it will never be over.

And now I involved Gloria. She may be dead because of me.

"How can I forgive myself?" I rub my forehead.

"This is *not* your fault, Aspen. You have to believe that. Tell me you believe that."

"But is it Gloria's fault? Just because she didn't report a conversation she heard after I disappeared?"

"That's what she told you, baby. You have no idea if it's the truth."

"But let's assume for a moment that it is the truth. This is a woman I knew—"

"Operative word being knew. You *knew* her. You don't *know* her."

"Okay. But let's forget about that for a moment and assume it's the truth. That all she did was fail to report a conversation she heard. Then I'm to blame. Because I got in touch with her, and I stirred the pot."

I rub my upper arms to ease the shivering—shivering that makes no sense in LA. The muscles beneath my flesh twitch, and my stomach tumbles. I'm going to be sick again...

"Damn it, Aspen. This is *not* your fault. I'm not going let you take any blame here. It's not a crime for you to want to find out who set the whole island thing in motion."

I pull away and meet his gaze, forcing my nausea back down my throat. "What do we do? Do we call 911?"

47

BUCK

I pull Aspen back toward me and kiss the top of her head. "Let me think."

She pulls away again. "What exactly is there to think about, Buck? Two people have been murdered in their sleep. We need to call 911."

"In a perfect world, yeah. We call 911. The problem is... If this *does* have something to do with the fact that you got in touch with Gloria, that means there are other things at work here."

"Yeah, it does. And if the police can find out who did this, it might lead us to who orchestrated my kidnapping."

God, I love this woman. But I've been around a block that she hasn't. She was held captive on an island, sure, and God knows she's been through hell. But she had to go inside herself to survive, and she's not thinking clearly right now.

The evil of people. The pure and unadulterated evil...

Aspen pulls her phone out of her pocket.

I grab her hand. "No, baby."

"We have to. We can't just let them...*rot* here. And what about the dog?"

She makes a good point about the dog.

"All right, here's what we do. We'll call 911 from their land-line. The call will be traced, and someone will come."

"Still... They won't do anything about the dog."

"We'll leave him inside. They'll find him, and someone will care for him."

"No! They'll leave him at a shelter where he'll be killed. No. Absolutely not." She picks up a squirming Edgar and brings him to her chest. "I won't let them. I won't let them kill this dog."

"We can't take him with us, baby."

"Why not?"

"Because if we do, someone will figure out that we were here."

"I don't care. I'm calling 911 now."

She yanks her hand away from me, letting Edgar go as well, and before I can stop her, she's punching numbers into her phone.

I grab the phone out of her hand before she hits send, thank God. I brace myself, stay in control despite what I'm feeling, and force my voice to remain calm.

"Aspen, listen to me."

"Give me my phone."

"Listen to me, baby."

"No. Give me my phone, Buck. You can't treat me like this. I'm not a fucking child. Now give me my damned phone!"

I shove the phone in my back pocket. Then I grab both her arms. "Listen to me. We broke in. If you call the police from your phone, they will trace your phone. They will have your number, and they will know we were here. They will know we broke in. That's a crime, baby. You know this. You know I'm right."

She leans into me then. "But the dog..."

I kiss the top of her head. "I wish we could take him. I do. I don't want to leave him. But we have to get out of here. And we have to get out of here now."

"So you'll dial 911 from the landline?"

"I will. But then we leave quickly. We have to make sure no one sees us."

"All right. I just have to know that Edgar's going to be all right."

"Edgar will be fine." I kiss her hair again and then I hand her the key fob. "Go out to the car. Get in and wait for me. If I don't come out within five minutes—and I'm serious—get the hell out of here."

"I'm not leaving without you."

I kiss her then. Hard. With a whole lot of tongue and whole lot of passion.

With a whole lot of love. Her safety is all that matters.

I don't want to stop the kiss, but I force myself. I gaze at her—at her beautiful, terror-stricken eyes.

"Go. Please. Give me five minutes."

Her lips tremble as she takes the key fob. "All right."

I nod and give her a little shove. She heads down the short hallway through the living area and out the door.

Once she's gone, I steel myself.

For the last few minutes, I've known.

We are not alone in this house.

"All right." I pull my Glock out of the holster. "Show yourself, you fucking coward."

It's a feeling. Instinct. I heard a few creaks, but this is an older home, and older homes creak.

Still, I know.

"Get the fuck out here," I say again, this time through gritted teeth. "Show yourself, you fucking psychopath."

Again, no response. I look down at Edgar who has stopped barking for a moment.

"You have to lead me to them, pup."

But Edgar only runs back into the bedroom, jumps on the bed, and tries to rouse his owners.

I follow him to the bedroom, check the closet and the adjoining bath.

Nothing.

Maybe my instinct is off. It wouldn't be the first time I've trusted my instinct and nothing panned out.

I only gave Aspen five minutes, and that's fine. Even if I'm still looking around in here, she'll leave and be safe. I hated lying to her—telling her I'd call 911 when I had no intention of doing so.

The bedroom seems to be clear, so I slink into the second bedroom. Edgar doesn't follow me. He stays with his owners' bodies.

The second bedroom closet is clear. There is no third bedroom. I check every other crevice I can find. The coat closet in the living room, the pantry in the kitchen.

There's no second floor, and there's no basement.

Damn it. The house appears to be clean.

I still have about thirty seconds to get to Aspen in the car. Then I look at Edgar, who has left the bedroom and is scurrying at my feet, barking.

"I don't know, boy. I think you and I might be hearing things."

I'm ready to leave, to join Aspen in the car and get out of here, when her voice echoes in my head.

We can't leave him here. He'll starve.

"Damn it, you dumb dog." I lean down and pet his soft head.

I'll find the landline phone. I'll dial 911. That way someone will come, and the dog will not starve. God, I hope he doesn't end up in a shelter.

"Fuck it all." I scoop him into my arms and head toward the front door.

48

ASPEN

Five minutes pass.

Then ten.

Buck, please, I beg him in my mind. *Please come out here. Please come back to me.*

I'm already five minutes past his limit.

Five minutes more. I'll give him five minutes more.

Tick. Tock. Tick. Tock.

The invisible clock ticks inside my mind.

When my five minutes are up—making fifteen minutes total—I press the start button on the car.

Where do I go? Back to the hotel?

No. I go to the only place I know where I can find help.

I plug Katelyn's address into the GPS, and I'm off.

LA traffic is the worst, especially heading toward the beach on a beautiful morning. It takes over an hour to make it to Katelyn's house. I screech to a halt and run to the door.

I bang on it. I bang on it relentlessly. Jed barks behind the door.

Until finally—

The door opens, and Luke stands there, stroking Jed's head.

"Aspen? What's the matter?"

"Help me. You've got to help me. Please."

"Come in. Come in."

I follow him inside.

"What's wrong? Where's Buck?"

I can't speak. I can barely breathe. My breath is coming in rapid pants.

"Calm down."

"Katelyn," I rasp out. "Where's Katelyn?"

"She's upstairs. I'll get her, okay?"

"Yes. Katelyn. Please."

But instead of going upstairs, he walks into the kitchen. He comes back with a small paper lunch bag.

"Breathe into this. It will help."

Right. Paper bag. Hyperventilating. Whatever. But I obey him. I breathe in and out into the paper bag. And to my surprise, it does help. I'm still breathing hard, but at least I can get a full breath now.

A few moments later, Katelyn comes running down the stairs with Luke.

"Aspen! What's wrong?"

I just nod, still breathing in and out into the bag.

"Easy," she says. "Okay. Breathe in. Breathe out."

Her gentle voice calms me. Finally I remove the bag.

"Tell us. Tell us what happened." She leads me to a sofa where we sit down.

Tears stream from my face as I relay the story in a trembling voice while I constantly try to brush the shivers from my arms. Gloria Delgado and her husband. Throat slit. Buck. Five minutes. Fifteen minutes.

"All right," Katelyn says. "We should call the police. Right, Luke?"

Luke doesn't reply at first. Then— "I'm not sure that's the best idea."

I widen my eyes. "Buck said he'd call 911 from their landline."

Luke shakes his head and wrinkles his forehead. "Really? Because from what I know about Buck, he probably thought that wasn't a good idea."

"That's what he said. He didn't think it was a good idea, but he promised me. He wouldn't lie to me."

Luke doesn't respond.

"No," I say. "You're thinking he'd lie to me. He didn't. He did *not* lie to me."

"I don't think he would lie to you intentionally, Aspen." Luke pushes at his hair. "But you have to consider that there's a reason why he wanted you to leave after five minutes."

"Why? What could the reason be?"

"I don't know what the specific reason could've been," Luke says, "but he was protecting you."

"I don't want him to protect me. I want him *with* me."

Katelyn grabs my hand. "What can I do for you? Maybe a drink of cool water? A glass of wine?"

"No. Nothing."

"Get her a glass of water," Luke says. "It will help."

Katelyn nods and hurries into the kitchen. A moment later she comes back with a glass of tepid water. No ice.

I'm thankful for it. I down the whole thing.

I didn't realize how thirsty I was.

"You're dehydrated," Luke says. "That's why I asked Katelyn to get the water."

"Please help me," I say. "Please find Buck."

"Of course we'll help," Katelyn says. "Won't we, Luke?"

"Absolutely. I owe Buck a lot, so I'll do anything you need me to do."

"That's just it," I say. "I don't *know* what we should do. You need to tell *me*."

"First thing is, I will go to this Gloria Delgado's house," Luke says.

"Yes. Let's leave now."

He shakes his head. "No. You need to stay here with Katelyn."

"Luke," Katelyn says, "we want to go with you."

"First of all, I can't risk anything happening to either of you," he says. "And second, Buck told you to leave for a reason, Aspen. He didn't want you there. And that means he was expecting that something might go wrong."

"I don't care. I want to be with him."

"He would want you safe. That's why you're going to stay here with Katelyn where you're safe."

"Wait just a minute," Katelyn intervenes. "I want *you* safe too, Luke. We've been through too much. I can't lose you."

He touches her cheek, much the same way Buck touches mine.

"I'll come back to you. I will always come back to you."

"How can you make that promise?"

"Because that's how much I love you, Katelyn. You and I have both already been through hell and we're meant to be together. We're meant to be happy. I won't risk that."

His words calm Katelyn. I can see it on her face as her features soften.

"If you're sure," she says. "If you're sure it's best."

"It is. I need to do this. Not just for Aspen but for Buck."

She nods, her lips trembling. "I understand." She gazes at

the diamond on her left hand. "Don't forget. Don't forget where your forever lies."

He kisses her lips. "I could never."

Luke walks upstairs, and within a few minutes, he returns. I gasp as I see the pistol in a holster around his waist.

"Not a gun..."

"I hope I don't have to use it," he says. "Believe me. But I have to be prepared."

Katelyn and I grasp each other's hands.

Luke leaves the house through the back. A moment later, Katelyn and I watch out the window as he drives away in a black SUV.

"He never drives that car," Katelyn says. "He always drives his Tesla S."

I don't reply.

I don't want to think about what significance Luke's choice of car may have.

All I can think about is Buck, and how I have the sinking feeling I'll never see him again.

49

BUCK

Moreno! *Moreno, can you hear me?*

The words come from above me. They're fuzzy, hazy.

No one calls me Moreno. Everyone calls me Buck.

Moreno! Damn it, wake up!

A cloud surrounds me. A cloud of fog, lodged in my brain. My eyes... I want to open them, but I can't. Nothing but darkness exists in front of my face.

Darkness and those words—those words from far away.

Moreno! Moreno! Damn!

Something twitches in me. Like a nerve jumping in my fingers.

Then something against my neck.

Pulse. Good.

Am I moving? I feel like I'm moving, but that can't be.

Then what little consciousness I have fades.

~

WHEN I OPEN MY EYES, faces blur above me. All kinds of faces, and there's something on my nose.

No, no. What's going on?

Again, words.

Male, mid-thirties. Probable concussion, head lac. Pulse is strong, BP low.

I open my mouth to speak, but I can't. Something's covering it.

Oxygen.

Beautiful, sweet air.

Aspen? I try to choke out. But I can't speak.

Aspen, Aspen! Where's Aspen?

Then everything goes black again.

"MR. MORENO. Mr. Moreno can you hear me?"

The words hit my ears like a sonic boom. I wince.

"I hear you," I say, not recognizing my own voice.

"Good, good. He's conscious. And he knows who he is."

I open my eyes, but everything's blurry.

"You had a laceration on your forehead, and you lost some blood, but you're stable now. You also have a moderate concussion. But you know who you are. Do you know where you are?"

I try to move my head. Big mistake. I feel like a knife is stabbing me in my skull. "No. I don't."

"You're at the hospital, Mr. Moreno. Cedars-Sinai."

"How? How did I get here?"

"A man brought you in, but he left before we could get his name."

Come on mind, work. I was at Gloria Delgado's house. I sent Aspen to the car...

I searched the place, grabbed Edgar...

I don't remember anything after that.

"Aspen! Where's Aspen?"

"I don't know. We can call her. Is that your wife?"

Aspen. I want Aspen. I want Aspen safe.

"Mr. Moreno? Do you have her number?"

"My phone. It's in my phone."

"All right. We'll check your phone."

Thank God. Check my phone. Find Aspen. I love Aspen.

"What happened to me?"

"Someone hit you on the head, enough to knock you unconscious. We stitched up your head wound. But like I said you did lose some blood. You need to rest."

Rest.

Rest sounds sublime.

Rest is where Aspen is.

I let my eyes close.

50

ASPEN

"I want to go see him," I say to Luke.

"I know you do. But it's best that we all lie low right now. I have contacts at the hospital, and he's stable. His injuries were not life-threatening. He'll be fine."

Every nerve in my body is jumping. Staying here? When Buck needs me? Not an option. "He needs me. He'll want to know that I'm safe."

"He will know. Like I said, I have contacts at the hospital. Once he's lucid, they have instructions to let him know that you're safe with Katelyn and me."

"I don't understand. Why are you being so cautious?"

"Because that's how Buck would want me to be."

I bite my lip. Luke is no doubt right. Through this whole thing, Buck has protected me at all costs. Even when I've made it very difficult for him.

"I just wish I could see him. Hold his hand."

"I know you do," Katelyn says. "But you need to trust Luke. He knows what he's doing."

Luke. Katelyn trusts him. In a strange way, so does Buck. I

have no choice. I must trust him as well.

Hours have passed. It's evening now. Luke is in his office, working apparently.

Katelyn and I sit in the back, sipping water, not talking.

"Until finally— "You need to eat something, Aspen."

"I can't. I feel sick. Anything I put in my mouth will come right back up."

"Just some crackers or something. It will help the nausea."

"I don't think it will."

"Does anything sound good to you?"

I shake my head. "Nothing."

I take a sip of my water and then jerk when Luke comes out on the patio.

"Good news. I heard from my contact at the hospital. Buck is awake, stable, and the message has been delivered. He knows that you're safe with Katelyn and me, Aspen."

"Stable? He's stable?"

"Yes. He'll be released tomorrow or the next day."

"What do I do?"

"Stay here with us," Katelyn says. "Right Luke?"

"Absolutely. We have plenty of room here, and we have top-notch security."

Top-notch security.

That means...

That means Luke thinks I may be in danger.

"What about Gloria? And Brian?"

"Aspen, I couldn't alert the authorities," Luke says. "I had to get Buck out of there and to the hospital."

"So they're still lying there? What about the dog?"

"Aspen..."

"No! That poor little dog! We can't leave him there to

starve to death! You wouldn't leave Jed, would you?"

"All right." Luke sighs. "I'll go get the dog."

"Is it safe?" Katelyn asks.

"I can do it. I know how to get in and out of a place undetected."

"If you're sure," Katelyn says.

"I'm sure."

"Okay." Katelyn says. "You'd better not end up in the hospital too."

"I won't. I promise."

Luke makes a lot of promises to Katelyn. Promises he can't actually know whether he can keep. Or does he? Does he still have contacts in the drug world? I don't want to know.

All I want is for Buck to come back to me, healthy and safe.

And Edgar... That silly little pup. I just can't bear the thought of him starving alone with his owners dead in their bed. Or being put down at a shelter.

It's silly, I know, but some part of me feels that if I can save that dog, everything will be okay.

KATELYN SITS, quiet, stroking Jed's soft head. Luke left an hour go to fetch Edgar.

I can hardly look at my friend. My request put her fiancé in danger.

Another hour passes.

Then another.

Katelyn will never speak to me again if Luke doesn't come back.

Neither of us can sleep, neither of us can eat.

It's after midnight now, and—

The back door opens, and a barking Edgar runs toward me. He and Jed check each other out.

I heave a sigh of relief, as Katelyn launches herself into Luke's arms.

"What took you so long? I've been so worried."

"I'm sorry, baby. I didn't want to worry you, but I took advantage of the time I had to case the place."

"No one saw you today?"

"No, I was very careful. I parked two blocks away and sneaked in the back. It was dark, and I made sure no one was around."

"Thank God," Katelyn nuzzles her head in Luke's shoulder.

I want to ask him what he found. I want to ask who might have done this to Buck.

But I stay quiet, let him and Katelyn have their time right now.

I take Edgar into the kitchen to get him some water. I find Jed's kibble and give Edgar a small portion. "Tomorrow I'll go to the store and get you some treats, okay?"

He ignores me as he guzzles down the food.

Luke comes in the kitchen to find me. "We need to talk, Aspen."

My stomach drops.

"No. Is it Buck? He's okay. Please tell me he's okay."

"Yes, Buck is okay. I got an update from my contact. He's sleeping soundly and his vitals are strong."

"Thank God." A sigh of relief whooshes out of me like a gust of wind.

"No, we need to talk about what I found at Gloria's house."

I nod. I'm exhausted, but I won't be able to sleep anyway. "Tell me."

He takes me to the family room, and I sit down on the couch. Katelyn sits next to me, and Luke sits on her other side, turning to face both of us.

"When I got to the house, the bodies—"

I wince.

"I mean Gloria and her husband... They weren't there."

I drop my jaw.

"Sometime between the time I got Buck out of there and took him to the hospital and when I went back to pick up Edgar, someone moved the bodies."

"What does that mean?" Katelyn asks.

"It means someone took away the evidence. The place was clean. There was absolutely no evidence of blood anywhere."

"But there was so much blood on the bed, and some of it had seeped onto the carpet."

"Cleaners," Luke says. "Professional cleaners. They can get blood out of anything. There is absolutely no evidence that anyone died in that room or anywhere in the house."

"That's why you were gone so long," Katelyn said.

"Yes. I told you I wanted to case the place. Cleaners had been there, so I had to look even more thoroughly. See if I could find anything they might've missed."

"But you didn't find anything." I say.

"No, I didn't."

"But Edgar was still there."

"He was outside. Whoever had been there put him outside."

"But he was inside when you left with Buck, right?" I ask.

"Yes. He was. And I left him inside with a full bowl of

water and a full bowl of food."

Luke goes up a notch in my mind then. He didn't rescue Edgar while he was there, but he did make sure he wouldn't starve for the next few days.

"What does it all mean?" Katelyn asks.

"It means were dealing with professionals. Someone with a lot of money and a lot of clout had Gloria and Brian taken care of."

"Who?" I ask. "Who would've done this?"

"I don't know. But I will find out. For you and for Buck. I owe him."

Katelyn is rigid next to me, and I know exactly what she's thinking.

She loves me, and she cares about Buck because I care about him. She cares about Buck because he helped her when they were both being held by the drug lord.

But her first loyalty is to her fiancé, to Luke.

She doesn't want him in danger.

And now...he's going to be in danger.

Because of me.

I don't know what to say. I could tell Luke to stay out of it. That once Buck is released from the hospital, we'll go back to Manhattan and forget all about this.

But I can't.

Someone tried to harm Buck. Someone killed Gloria and her husband.

And it's all because of me.

This is my fault.

I need Luke's help. I need Luke's help to put a stop to all of it.

"Katelyn..." I begin.

She turns to me, swallows back a sob. "No, Aspen. Don't

go there."

"I'm sorry."

"What happened to you and what happened to me. None of it is our fault."

"I understand that. But I'll let this go. I'll let it go for you. For Luke. Buck and I can go back to Manhattan. I don't need to know who was behind this. All I really need is to get on with my life."

Katelyn gazes at me. She wants to take me up on my offer. I can tell, but she won't.

She won't because she meets her fiancé's gaze.

And his blue eyes—they tell a different story.

He will *not* let this go. His reasons are somewhat of a mystery to me, but they strengthen my resolve.

I harden. I harden into a freaking statue.

Buck could have been killed. Gloria and Brian *were* killed.

Whoever sealed my fate those years ago is still out there. I *will* track them down. Not only for me, but for the man I love.

Yes, the man I *love*.

The confession inside my mind doesn't surprise me.

It's there.

As if it's always been there and it always will be.

I love Buck Moreno.

So I'm in. I'm all in. I gather every ounce of courage, mettle, and strength I possess, and let the fierce determination surge through me like fire.

Hello, old friend.

Garnet is all in too.

THE STORY of Aspen and Buck continues in *Buck*, coming July 31, 2022!

A NOTE FROM HELEN

Dear Reader,

Thank you for reading *Garnet*. If you want to find out about my current backlist and future releases, please visit my website, like my Facebook page, and join my mailing list. If you're a fan, please join my Facebook street team (Hardt & Soul) to help spread the word about my books. I regularly do awesome giveaways for my street team members.

If you enjoyed the story, please take the time to leave a review. I welcome all feedback.

I wish you all the best!

Helen

Sign up for my newsletter here:

http://www.helenhardt.com/signup

ACKNOWLEDGMENTS

Thank you so much to the following individuals who helped make *Moonstone* shine: Karen Aguilera, Linda Pantlin Dunn, Serena Drummond, Christie Hartman, Kim Killion, Eric McConnell, and Angela Tyler.

ABOUT THE AUTHOR

#1 *New York Times,* #1 *USA Today,* and #1 *Wall Street Journal* bestselling author Helen Hardt's passion for the written word began with the books her mother read to her at bedtime. She wrote her first story at age six and hasn't stopped since. In addition to being an award-winning author of romantic fiction, she's a mother, an attorney, a black belt in Taekwondo, a grammar geek, an appreciator of fine red wine, and a lover of Ben and Jerry's ice cream. She writes from her home in Colorado, where she lives with her family. Helen loves to hear from readers.

Please sign up for her newsletter here:
http://www.helenhardt.com/signup
Visit her here:
http://www.helenhardt.com